Quests of Doom 4

Between a Rock and a Charred Place

Author	Editor	Front Cover Art
Tom Knauss	Jeff Harkness	Artem Shukaev
Developer	**Swords & Wizardry Conversion**	**Interior Art**
Patrick N. Pilgrim	Jeff Harkness	Blake Wilkie
Producer	**Layout and Graphic Design**	**Cartography**
Bill Webb	Charles A. Wright	Robert Altbauer

FROG GOD GAMES IS

CEO	Frog V	Customer Service Manager
Bill Webb	Patrick N. Pilgrim	Krista Webb
Creative Director: Swords & Wizardry	**Art Director**	**Zach of All Trades**
Matthew J. Finch	Charles A. Wright	Zach Glazar
Creative Director: Pathfinder Roleplaying Game	**Developers**	**Final Boss**
Greg A. Vaughan	John Ling and Patrick N. Pilgrim	Skeeter Green

ADVENTURES
WORTH
WINNING

FROG
GOD
GAMES

Other Products from Frog God Games

You can find these product lines and more at our website, **froggodgames.com**, and on the shelves of many retail game stores. Superscripts indicate the available game systems: "PF" means the Pathfinder Roleplaying Game, "5e" means Fifth Edition, and "S&W" means *Swords & Wizardry*. If there is no superscript it means that it is not specific to a single rule system.

GENERAL RESOURCES

Swords & Wizardry Complete [S&W]
The Tome of Horrors Complete [PF, S&W]
Tome of Horrors 4 [PF, S&W]
Tome of Adventure Design
Monstrosities [S&W]
Bill Webb's Book of Dirty Tricks
Razor Coast: Fire as She Bears [PF]
Book of Lost Spells [5e, PF]
Fifth Edition Foes [5e]
The Tome of Blighted Horrors [5e, PF, S&W]
Book of Alchemy* [5e, PF, S&W]

THE LOST LANDS

Rappan Athuk [PF, S&W]
Rappan Athuk Expansions Vol. I [PF, S&W]
The Slumbering Tsar Saga [PF, S&W]
The Black Monastery [PF, S&W]
Cyclopean Deeps Vol. I [PF, S&W]
Cyclopean Deeps Vol. II [PF, S&W]
Razor Coast [PF, S&W]
Razor Coast: Heart of the Razor [PF, S&W]
Razor Coast: Freebooter's Guide to the Razor Coast [PF, S&W]
LL0: The Lost Lands Campaign Setting* [5e, PF, S&W]
LL1: Stoneheart Valley [PF, S&W]

LL2: The Lost City of Barakus [PF, S&W]
LL3: Sword of Air [PF, S&W]
LL4: Cults of the Sundered Kingdoms [PF, S&W]
LL5: Borderland Provinces [5e, PF, S&W]
LL6: The Northlands Saga Complete [PF, S&W]
LL7: The Blight [5e, PF, S&W]
LL8: Bard's Gate [5e, PF, S&W]
LL9: Adventures in the Borderland Provinces [5e, PF, S&W]

QUESTS OF DOOM

Quests of Doom (Vol. 1) [5e]
Quests of Doom (Vol. 2) [5e]
Quests of Doom (includes the 5e Vol. 1 and 2, but for PF and S&W only) [PF, S&W]
Quests of Doom 2 [5e]
Quests of Doom 3 [5e, S&W]
Quests of Doom 4* [5e, PF, S&W]

PERILOUS VISTAS

Dead Man's Chest (pdf only) [PF]
Dunes of Desolation [PF]
Fields of Blood [PF]
Mountains of Madness [PF]
Marshes of Malice [PF]

* (forthcoming from **Frog God Games**)

Table of Contents

Between a Rock and a Charred Place

A fiery blast tore through their ranks
And buckled their vulnerable flanks,
The hobgoblins burned with eyes of flame,
Still they came, still they came!

— **"Varrandungen"**
an epic poem translated from the original Dwarven

Between a Rock and a Charred Place is an adventure for 6th-level characters that thrusts them into the middle of an epic confrontation between the dwarves of the Stoneheart Mountains and the hobgoblins just beyond their borders. Under their new leadership, the hobgoblin warmongers deploy an innovative grand strategy: to forge an alliance with one of the dwarves' old enemies and a traitor in their foes' midst. The dwarves' dominance over the region and very survival hangs in the balance if the characters cannot thwart the monsters' ambitious plans.

Adventure Background

The frenetic beat of war drums pounds in the heart of every hobgoblin warrior. The martial rhythm urges these aggressive humanoids to new conquests and greater brutality. Their voracious appetite for spilling blood and their compulsive need to subjugate other sentient beings to their will perpetuates a never-ending state of war against their unwilling neighbors. Many of these conflicts rage for centuries as the forces of civilization struggle to keep the expansionistic hobgoblin armies at bay. For dwarves, the battle against the hobgoblins and their malevolent kin is an indelible way of life. From an early age, dwarves learn how to combat these hated foes, and most get the opportunity to put their lessons into practice on the battlefield. Nowhere is this truer than in the Stoneheart Mountains.

The mountain dwarves of Clan Craenog who dominate much of the eastern and central Stoneheart Mountains always keep a wary eye pointed north toward the Starcrag Range and, more specifically, the hobgoblin citadels of Exor, Smashed Skull, and Hollow Bone. In spite of several impressive victories by both sides over the past several hundred years, territorial gains are invariably short-lived. The two foes remain locked in a virtual stalemate. For the most part, the leaders on both sides grudgingly accept the status quo. However, a young and remarkably intelligent hobgoblin warlord aspires to finally break the deadlock and assume supremacy over the Stoneheart Mountains.

From his stronghold of Exor, the new hobgoblin warlord Grugdour believes that the complacent dwarves are ripe for conquest. The dwarves' lack of a king fuels rumors of discontent among several prominent families within the court of Erod Flan, the clan's capital. Grugdour senses weakness and disunity, especially in light of the troubles experienced at Burvaadun, and he intends to exploit the situation. Hobgoblins are not renowned for diplomacy and subterfuge. In the minds of his predecessors, victory was won only on the battlefield. They would happily launch a bloody frontal assault against the heavily fortified dwarven citadel of Tyr Whin, the clan's only significant military presence in the north. The tactically brilliant and charismatic hobgoblin warlord realizes that it takes more than military might to wrest the critically important military installation from the hands of his enemies. In his mind, it is better to share glory with others than taste defeat alone.

With that philosophy in mind, Grugdour knows that his hobgoblins are not the dwarves' only enemy. Several decades earlier, the dwarves of Erod Flan eradicated a clan of dark folk, a humanoid race with a longstanding grudge against the dwarves, from the abandoned quartz mine beneath the citadel's foundation. At least, that is what the dwarves thought. The dark folk's leader, a dark caller named Rogvörn, led a ragtag handful of dark creepers and dark stalkers into a hidden chamber that the dwarves failed to find. Since their devastating defeat, they have slowly and stealthily rebuilt and repopulated the subterranean complex beneath the citadel, waiting for the perfect opportunity to exact their revenge.

Hours of Discontent

Fortunately for Grogdour, Clan Craenog is not fully united behind its current high thane. After the disappearance and presumed death of King Kroma during the Battle of Tsar three centuries ago, the surviving dwarves left the title of king vacant and instead elevated Kroma's first cousin, Om, to the position of high thane. Naturally, some disagreed with this decision. Om's older, cousin Garnock, a dwarf poorly suited to diplomacy and rule, demanded that his kin crown him high thane. The clan's most influential dwarves chaffed at the idea of bestowing the title to a bumbling lout. No one supported the universally disliked Garnock in his bid to assume clan leadership. The bitter old dwarf vehemently protested the perceived slight until his dying breath almost two centuries later. Before succumbing to old age, the venerable dwarf married a dwarven woman more than two hundred years his junior. The short-lived relationship produced his only child — the surprisingly bright and affable Blassian. In fact, the youngster was so different from the unpopular Garnock that many of his relatives were certain that someone else actually fathered the impressive boy. Still, Blassian shares one common trait with his father: He wants to rule Clan Craenog as Kroma's rightful heir.

Though more charismatic and intelligent than his gruff, ignorant father, Blassian's political maneuverings and machinations appear to be all for naught. The popular dwarf is widely respected within the clan, yet his elusive goal now seems completely unattainable considering that Om's oldest son and the current high thane, Kaelan, along with his two younger brothers, two sons, and four grandsons all stand in his way. Despite outward appearances, Blassian's fidelity to the clan is a ruse. He is loyal only to one person — himself. Blassian greatly resents how Om and his descendants treated his admittedly boorish father. Now convinced that he cannot attain his desired goal through peaceful means, the desperate and ambitious dwarf looked elsewhere for aid.

Strangest Bedfellows

Distance and race separate Rogvörn, Grogdour, and Blassian, yet they share one faith that binds them together. Outwardly, each worships the traditional gods of their people. However, in secret, the diverse trio worships Hecate's daughter, Mirkeer, Goddess of Shadows and the Night. Their divine mistress heard their prayers and united the three conspirators using a bloody bones servant to act as their intermediary. In spite of their differences in language, culture, and ideology, Blassian found willing allies in Grugdour, his equally smart and determined hobgoblin counterpart, and Rogvörn, the dark caller responsible for saving the dark folk beneath Erod Flan. United by their common belief, the devious trio concocted a sinister plot to accomplish all of their goals in one fell swoop.

The masterful scheme has several moving parts. Rogvörn intends to use a pocket of volatile natural gas to wipe out the high thane's entire family during a ceremony to honor the characters' recent actions on the Feirgotha

Plateau. Naturally, Blassian skips the event, allowing him to survive the devastating blast, which leaves him as the most logical choice to succeed his cousin as Clan Craenog's undisputed high thane. In accordance with their carefully crafted plan, the dwarves' new leader urges his kin to venture into the depths below Erod Flan and avenge their fallen high thane. After the dwarves sustain significant casualties in the trapped underground tunnels and chambers, the newly crowned high thane cedes the territory beneath Erod Flan to the conniving dark caller and his dark creeper servitors. Meanwhile, in response to the massive explosion, Blassian summons reinforcements from Tyr Whin, leaving the important outpost at less than half its original strength. As the dwarven relief force marches across the Stoneheart Mountains toward the clan's capital, Grugdour's hobgoblins launch a surprise assault against the significantly weakened citadel. If all goes according to design, Rogvörn and the dark folk would rule the underground realm below Erod Flan, Blassian would become high thane and assume leadership over Clan Craenog, and Grugdour would add an important symbolic and tactical piece to his expanding kingdom. Mirkeer and her servants would claim secret dominion over an enormous swath of the central Stoneheart Mountains.

Of course, the characters are hopefully there to prove once again that the best laid plans of dwarves, hobgoblins, dark folk, and a secretive goddess all go awry. (The characters' journey to Tyr Whin and their battle against the hobgoblins and their ambitious overlord appears in the adventure *War of Shadows*.)

Adventure Synopsis

If the characters participated in the adventure *A Little Knowledge*, the Referee may segue directly into this adventure by having a column of dwarven reinforcements escort the characters from the distant garrison of Burvaadun to Erod Flan approximately 100 miles away to meet with the high thane. Alternately, Clan Craenog's high thane invites the characters to the fortress to honor them for their actions on another matter of importance to the mountain dwarves.

During the ceremony, Rogvörn and the dark folk ignite a pocket of methane gas that causes a loud and powerful explosion that shakes the audience hall to its foundations. Though the blast causes a considerable amount of structural damage and some injuries, the scheming dark caller and his minions fail in their bid to kill the high thane and his immediate family. The startled high thane again asks the characters to risk their lives and venture into the tunnels beneath Erod Flan to prevent another catastrophe and unmask the culprits. Blassian, one of the conspirators, needs additional time to devise an alternate plan, so he offers to lead the expedition into the underground complex where he hopes to lure the characters to their doom.

The characters may either enter the dark folk's complex through the abandoned quartz mine beneath Erod Flan or by excavating tons of rock and stone from the blast site and infiltrate their lair through the proverbial backdoor. The dark folk expect the dwarves to counterattack, and are well prepared for the dwarves (and possibly the characters). Lethal traps and hand-chosen guardians lie in wait throughout the mine's claustrophobic tunnels and chambers. Of course, Blassian, the high thane's supposedly loyal subject and the characters' alleged ally, intervenes whenever possible to thwart the characters' interference with the grand scheme. The clan's would-be ruler shows his true colors at the most opportune moment, joining with his dark folk allies or their minions to prevent the characters from ruining his plans.

After the characters successfully stymie the traitorous dwarf, they must still contend with the surviving dark folk and their minions on their home turf. Deadly traps and volatile pockets of explosive gas make their task even more difficult. As the characters explore the dark folk's alien world and encounter its leader caste, they learn of Grugdour's involvement in this elaborate plot and the hobgoblins' planned assault against Tyr Whin. In the depths below the dwarven citadel, the characters encounter one of the plot's architects, the vengeful Rogvörn. The dark folk's unquestioned leader and Mirkeer's bloody bones servant sense that their original plan failed, so they scramble to set off another devastating detonation that could potentially level wide swaths of the city. If the characters cannot stop him, hundreds and perhaps even thousands of dwarves may meet Dwerfater sooner than they intended.

Part I: Pomp and Circumstance

The adventure's opening scenes take place in the dwarven citadel of Erod Flan, first city of the Great Mountain Clan Craenog. In recognition of their services to Clan Craenog, the high thane personally invites the characters to attend a traditional dwarven feast followed by a ceremony granting them exalted status among the mountain dwarves. Before the festivities, the characters are free to briefly explore the citadel and restock their supplies and equipment or to gather vital information from the local residents that could aid them later in the adventure. After touring Erod Flan, the characters may interact with the high thane and his court throughout the extravagant meal. Then, as the high thane is about to grant the characters the lofty title "Brothers of the Thane," a powerful blast rips through the hall, collapsing parts of the ceiling and injuring some of the guests. The angered and concerned thane turns to the characters and asks them to unmask the responsible parties and prevent his fortress from coming to ruin.

Beginning the Adventure

The adventure may begin in any location under the dominion of Clan Craenog. However, the remote garrison of Burvaadun from the previous adventure is the most-logical starting point. It is preferential for the high thane to dispatch a contingent of his troops to notify the characters of his intention to honor them and then to escort them back to Erod Flan along the low-ways of the clan peaks, thus eliminating the need for random encounters on their trip to the clan's capital. Of course, it is possible to allow the characters to venture on their own to Erod Flan from another location somewhere in the Stoneheart Mountains.

Adventure Hooks

Between a Rock and a Charred Place begins in a rather innocuous way. The adventure starts with a happy occasion instead of the characters investigating a mysterious location or confronting a growing menace. The high thane invites them to attend a celebratory gathering held in their honor and to bestow an important title upon them. The three hooks presented below deliver the same message, yet each does so in a different manner. The Referee is free to use one of the following hooks or create one of his own to set the adventure's events into motion.

Heroes of Burvaadun

Characters who defeated Thanopsis and his undead legions at the behest of **Voorn Rockfeller** (Neutral male mountain dwarf fighter 3) must eventually return to Burvaadun to collect payment for their services and to inform **Thurn Rockfeller**, the garrison's commander, of their success. When the characters arrive at Burvaadun, Thurn hands them a message from Voorn asking them to remain at the garrison until the high thane's reinforcements finally arrive one week later. As promised, **Omgard Karskbit** (Lawful male mountain dwarf fighter 5) appears at the remote outpost along with 80 fresh dwarven soldiers under his command. Sixty of the troops join the survivors at the garrison along with several wagons stuffed with provisions and other critical supplies. Omgard tells the characters that the grateful high thane wants them to accompany him and 20 of his men back to Erod Flan for a banquet in their honor as well as to receive a special gift from Clan Craenog's leader. If the characters travel with Omgard and his soldiers, the overland trip takes a week to slog the roughly 100 miles back to Erod Flan.

Thurn Rockfeller, Male Mountain Dwarf Garrison Commander: HD 6; AC 4[15]; Atk hand axe (1d6+2), light crossbow (1d4+1); Move 9; Save 9; AL N; CL/XP 6/400; Special: +2 to hit and damage strength bonus, +4 saves vs.

magic, multiple attacks (6) vs. creatures with 1 or fewer HD, darkvision 60ft.

Equipment: chainmail, shield, hand axe, light crossbow, 20 bolts.

Long Days' Journey

Characters seeking to claim their compensation for retrieving one of the library's valuable tomes or solving the mystery surrounding the fate of the missing youngsters at the time of Arcady's collapse must return to one of the human settlements in either Miners' Refuge or another suitable lowlands location. Clan Craenog sends **Kellyn Cyanbrass** (Lawful female mountain dwarf ranger 4) and her band of 12 rangers to find the adventurers who saved the garrison of Burvaadun from certain destruction. Kellyn eventually tracks the characters to their current location and delivers the same message as her counterpart Omgard. She and her followers agree to escort the characters back to Erod Flan to attend the feast and ritual. Depending upon the characters' starting point, the journey can take anywhere from a few weeks to several months depending on where the characters are located when Kellyn finds them.

Enemy Mine

Clan Craenog has many bitter enemies: Humans, orcs, goblins, hobgoblins, elves, and giants rank at the top of their list. If the characters did not participate in the adventure *A Little Knowledge*, the high thane instead seeks to honor them for defeating one or more of the preceding foes at some other point in their adventuring career. Rather than directly summoning the characters to Erod Flan, the characters learn of the high thane's interest through a local settlement's rumor mill, a public announcement, or a display asking for information about the characters. The Referee may also choose an alternate means of notification. Without the benefit of an armed escort, it is best to use this hook only in close proximity to Erod Flan. Otherwise, the characters may have to negotiate several hundred miles of hostile territory without the protection afforded by traveling with a large group under the high thane's jurisdiction.

Erod Flan

Roughly 70 miles east of the Feirgotha Plateau, Clan Craenog's capital and most-formidable fortress is a monument to dwarven engineering and military planning. The citadel is centrally located in relation to the three vital mountain passes under the dwarves' control. It is nearly halfway between Baen's Pass and the Southern Pass. Pelivar Pass lies on the western boundary of the narrowest stretch of the Feirgotha Plateau due west from Erod Flan. Though most dwarves refer to Erod Flan as a citadel, the defensive bulwark is more than a military outpost. Aristocrats and soldiers need food, clothing, water, and an assortment of other goods just to meet their basic needs. They also require a vast and sophisticated infrastructure to produce and deliver these essential commodities among desolate mountain peaks and difficult terrain. Every profession typically found in larger rural settlements is well-represented in Clan Craenog's formidable capital.

First Impressions

The towering fortress of Erod Flan is an architectural marvel for peaceful visitors to behold. But the mighty citadel elicits images of sheer terror in the eyes and mind of an attacking warrior. Clan Craenog built the centerpiece of their kingdom atop an elongated mesa 7428ft above sea level. Sheer rock walls and cliffs make up much of the slope surrounding the elevated structure. An attacking army without significant magical resources or an innate ability to fly would find it nearly impossible to reach Erod Flan's forbidding walls by any means other than the two mountain passes that carve a negotiable path through the mountains bordering the citadel. One pass approaches the main gate from the east, whereas the other leads to a secondary entrance on the southeastern face. Both routes weave a gently sloping, meandering road through the rugged rocks. Hairpin turns and narrow stretches barely wide enough to accommodate two dwarves standing side-by-side mark each path. Of course, Erod Flan's builders intentionally designed the passes in this manner to prevent enemies from lugging heavy siege equipment up the mountainside and positioning these devices within feasible striking distance of its outer defenses. The Referee may read or paraphrase the following description of the fortress when the characters first set eyes upon the intimidating structure.

A pair of narrow, winding mountain passes carves a navigable pass through the treacherous stones and sheer surfaces that separate the base of a series of interconnected mountains from an elongated mesa at the summit. A mighty fortress with 30-foot-high walls and two gates dominates the roughly one-square-mile plateau. Numerous figures man parapets atop the walls, keeping a vigilant watch in every direction. Seven 60-foot-high towers are strategically positioned along the walls.

Erod Flan

Lawful large town

Government overlord
Population 4609 (4534 mountain dwarves, 75 halflings)
Notable NPCs
    Kaelan, High Thane of Clan Craenog (Lawful male mountain dwarf cleric of Dwerfater 7)
    Minchain Redash, Guard Captain (Neutral male mountain dwarf fighter 7)
    Edda Brittlestone, Quartermaster (Lawful female mountain dwarf expert 6)

The characters' escorts lead them through the southeastern gate and into Erod Flan proper. The dwarven citadel looks more like a walled, cosmopolitan settlement than a military installation. The Referee may read or paraphrase the following description detailing the sprawling compound.

In spite of the omnipresence of dwarven soldiers clad in heavy armor and carrying an arsenal of weapons, the immense citadel boasts all of the features typically found in a large settlement. Several hundred sheep, goats, and cattle graze in an enclosed pasture adjacent to at least 100 acres of open farmland. Numerous small homes and granaries dot the landscape. The dwarves in the high thane's service presumably dwell in two enormous barracks complexes. The larger structure dominates the northeastern quadrant of Erod Flan, and the smaller one is in the southeastern section adjacent to the military training grounds and the high thane's palace. Merchants, craftsmen and professionals sell their wares and their services in the bustling marketplace at the citadel's heart. In addition to housing their shops and offices, the businesses' proprietors and employees alike permanently live here as well.

The high thane keeps a tight schedule, so the characters cannot spend more than a few hours wandering through Erod Flan. As a rule of thumb, allow the characters 1d4 hours to explore Erod Flan before their audience with the high thane. Still, their brief foray through the streets and alleyways gives them enough time to pick up on some of the prevailing rumors and to restock their supplies.

General Features

Not surprisingly, dwarves dominate the citadel by an incredibly large margin. A small halfling community ekes out an existence manufacturing clever gadgets and plying trades useful to the dwarves. Erod Flan is almost evenly divided between its military and civilian population. The high thane's army boasts 2415 full-time professional soldiers. The majority man the walls and towers along the citadel's perimeter. Meanwhile, several hundred warriors constantly patrol the rugged mountains surrounding the settlement. These squadrons number between 20 and 40 soldiers, including at least one captain or watch officer. The troops usually spend at least a month in the untamed wilderness before returning home to the comparable safety of Erod Flan.

In addition to the regular army, 1155 civilians participate in monthly military exercises and are equipped and trained to serve their liege in an emergency. Still, the dwarven commanders know that infrequent drilling is not a substitute for actual combat experience. Few auxiliary troops have ever swung an axe at a live enemy or stared death in the face. In the minds of Erod Flan's commanders, deploying them in battle is a measure of last resort and not a tactical option.

Like most mountain dwarf communities, men outnumber women by a staggering five-to-one margin. Most dwarves sarcastically quip that it is easier to find a flawless pearl inside a wild boar's anus than it is to find a wife in Erod Flan. The fierce competition for a suitable mate combined with the effects of copious amounts of beer and frayed nerves provides the catalyst for the steady stream of fistfights and brawls within the citadel. Military leaders clearly understand the reasons for their troops' frustrations, but they must maintain order within the ranks and not excuse such behavior without disciplining the offenders.

Brief Tour

At first glance, Erod Flan appears no different than any other large town. It grows crops and raises livestock to feed and clothe its population. The central market (**Area D** on the map of Erod Flan), contains a diverse array of shops and businesses that cater to the visitors' every need. Yet, it differs from the conventional settlement in one important respect. The military is typically born from the need to protect the community. In Erod Flan, the community exists to support the army.

Still, the dwarven capital boasts the services and goods found in any commercial center. There are twelve taverns scattered throughout the citadel, including The Sharpened Axe, Dead Man's Hand, and Dwarves' Delight. These establishments serve soldiers and civilians alike. On the other hand, all of the proprietors who sell food, basic supplies and adventuring gear primarily serve the military's needs. **Edda Brittlestone** (Neutral female mountain dwarf expert 6) makes bulk purchases on behalf of the high thane's army at a significant discount to the clan. Of course, these businessmen peddle their wares to individuals as well. However, soldiers and civilians typically pay standard prices for equipment, whereas merchants always charge unfamiliar faces 1d4 x 10% more than their usual customers. Alchemical substances are available only at the Smoking Gnome's Tinker Shop. Located in the tiny halfling section of Erod Flan, the shop's eccentric owner, **Glarn Goldentoe** (Lawful male halfling magic-user 6) offers fair prices for his wondrous creations and poor advice for practically everything else.

Rumors in Erod Flan

Erod Flan's mighty walls are tall enough and strong enough to keep enemies at bay, but they would have to be 100 miles high to keep rumors out of the citadel. Reconnaissance missions and travelers ensure that a steady stream of news and stories enters the fortress on a regular basis. Merely conversing with Erod Flan's residents and soldiers is sufficient for each character to gain 1d3 of these rumors.

• Kaelan, the current high thane of Clan Craenog, is elderly and frail. He is Om's oldest living son at the venerable age of 269. Consensus holds that his older son Thron is next in line to rule the kingdom. Kaelan's two younger brothers still have a legitimate claim to succeed their sibling. However, neither has expressed any intention to do so after Kaelan's passing.

• Erod Flan boasts a standing army of 2500 well-trained professional soldiers with an auxiliary force of more than 1000 axes, swords, and crossbows.

• Over the last several months, Clan Craenog's dwarves have skirmished against small bands of goblins, hobgoblins, and orcs during their excursions into the Stoneheart Mountains.

• The hobgoblin strongholds of Exor, Bone Hollow, and Smashed Skull pose the greatest threat to Clan Craenog's dominance of the region. The highly disciplined and organized goblinoids can muster a combined force of 10,000 warriors. Fortunately, the hobgoblins are fractured and divided. Each of the three strongholds has its own warlord.

• Orcs are massing near the Southern Pass and appear poised to launch an assault against Burvaadun and the Fiergotha Plateau. They seem intent on returning to the Library of Arcady for some inexplicable reason. (This is a false rumor.)

• Brave adventurers recently saved the garrison of Burvaadun from certain destruction. The high thane invited them to Erod Flan to honor them for their heroism.

Greater Details

While there is no shortage of rumors in Erod Flan, some stories are more accessible than others. Characters intent on gathering more detailed information may interact with the local residents or recall tales they overheard or personally experienced at some point during their adventuring career. The Referee must exercise judgment when doling out these additional details. The common foot soldier may be a good source of information about present and past battles, but he is less likely to know anything about intrigues within the high thane's court.

Clan Craenog and Erod Flan

The characters may learn the following information about Clan Craenog and Erod Flan. Roll 1d20 once and give the characters all the information with the target number and below.

1d20	Result
10	Even Old High Thane Om's ascension to high thane did not go undisputed. His boorish older cousin, Garnock, vigorously protested being passed over in favor of his more tactful and widely respected younger cousin. Though he disputed this alleged injustice until his death, Kroma's family unanimously dismissed his claims and universally supported Om's succession. Kaelan is Om's oldest son.
16	Erod Flan is built atop a formerly active quartz mine. The dwarves depleted the mine's rich deposits, and abandoned it a few decades ago after encountering and defeating a small clan of dark folk who moved into the tunnels. The dwarves sealed the mine by deliberately collapsing the adit leading into it and casting powerful spells on the entrance.

Stoneheart Mountains

The characters may learn the following information about the surrounding Stoneheart Mountains. Roll 1d20 once and give the characters all the information with the target number and below.

1d20	Result
7	Miners dangerously close to Exor recently unearthed a vein of platinum. Tyr Whin sent 100 soldiers to the site to fend off the hobgoblins and allow the dwarves to extract the precious metal. As soon as the hobgoblins arrive in force, the miners intend to trap the mine. (This is a false rumor.)
10	Humans from the lowlands are attempting to resettle portions of the eastern Stoneheart Mountains. Their emissary offered the indigenous dwarves 100 pearls in exchange for several hundred square miles of land. The high thane is currently contemplating the proposal. (This is a false rumor.)
13	A young and energetic hobgoblin named Grugdour recently assumed control of the citadel of Exor. He is more intelligent than his peers and openly stated that he plans to unite the hobgoblins and wrest the Stoneheart Mountains from Clan Craenog. Despite his boasts, there is no increased hobgoblin activity in the area.
16	Truvven Blackgranite, Kaelan's most-trusted son-in-law commands Tyr Whin, the clan's northernmost citadel. He has 1000 trained dwarves at his disposal. Truvven recently asked Kaelan to transfer an additional 500 soldiers from Erod Flan to Tyr Whin. The high thane denied his request.

Audience with the High Thane

Given the high thane's advanced age and declining health, his staff and advisors waste no time preparing for the banquet and ceremony scheduled to take place either at noon or in the early evening, depending upon the time that the characters arrived in Erod Flan. As previously mentioned, these arrangements likely allow the characters to explore the citadel for a few hours before meeting Clan Craenog's ailing ruler. When they arrive at the high thane's palace (**Area F** on the map of Erod Flan), a retinue of six dwarven soldiers clad in breastplates and armed with ornately decorated longswords greets them and escorts them through the labyrinth of corridors into the high thane's banquet chamber. When the characters arrive, the Referee may read or paraphrase the following description.

Several dozen dwarves attired in fine robes stand at attention and raise their silver tankards. In unison they shout, "In the hall of the High Thane, there are none but brothers. In the eyes of all dwarves, there are no others. Bring glory, duty, and honor to our table. Fight to the end until no longer able. Hail Kaelan, High Thane of Clan Craenog! Hail our honored guests, now blood of his line!" A thunderous ovation echoes through the massive banquet chamber, as servants scramble to bring roasted meats, fragrant cheeses, and other dwarven delicacies to the hungry guests seated at long oak tables in front of a wizened dwarf dozing off on an ornately carved onyx throne. The elderly dwarf wears the trappings of royalty, including a silver-and-gold crown, a golden amulet, and elegant silk clothing. His trembling hands grip the handle of an ivory cane.

The soldiers who accompanied the characters depart, and a handsome, robust dwarf emerges from the crowd to greet them. He introduces himself as the high thane's older son, **Thron** (Lawful male mountain dwarf fighter 5). He discreetly whispers to the characters and instructs them to stand behind him and repeat what he does as they approach his father **Kaelan** (Neutral male mountain dwarf cleric of Dwerfater 7). When they reach the throne, Thron drops to one knee and uses a quiet hand gesture to tell the characters to do the same.

With the entire hall watching, Thron says, "We kneel as servants and rise as equals." If the characters do not get the hint and recite the same words, Thron looks back at them and signals to them to repeat after him. Thron returns to his feet, walks over to the throne and bows in front of the high thane. He places his arms on the high thane's shoulders and says, "I stand with you, my brother, wherever the path may lead us. I stand beside you, my brother, wherever darkness prevails. I stand in front of you, my brother, where others dare not go. Let neither time nor distance separate us, for the same blood flows through our veins until we pass onto the next world." Once again, Thron instructs each character to repeat the oath of brotherhood.

After the final character recites his vows, the feeble thane leans heavily on his cane and rises to his unsteady feet. He declares in a weak voice, "Though water washes all things away, blood endures forever. In the eyes of gods and mortals, we are now kin, born of the same union." With those words, the high thane gently falls back into his seat, and the hall again erupts into a mixture of song and applause. The high thane's statement concludes the Brothers of the High Thane ceremony, and the characters are invited to participate in the ensuing festivities.

Feast

The high thane's entire family attends the ceremony, including his older son Thron, younger son **Rawdwr** (Lawful male mountain dwarf ranger 4) and Kaelan's two younger brothers, **Egan** (Neutral male mountain dwarf aristocrat 5) and **Hangel** (Neutral male mountain dwarf fighter 6). In addition, Thron's three sons, **Eara** (Neutral male mountain dwarf thief 3), **Ghadra** (Neutral male mountain dwarf cleric of Dwerfater 4), **Gwydre** (Lawful male dwarf paladin of Dwerfater 3), and Rawdwr's only son, **Braydon** (Lawful male mountain dwarf barbarian 3), are there as well. Kaelan's two daughters and his children's spouses, granddaughters, and nieces are spread throughout the crowd.

At this point in Kaelan's life, the trappings of wealth and power can no longer conceal the ravages of age. The pious high thane remains one of

present when the dwarves defeated the dark folk in the abandoned mine shafts. He describes his foes as ragged, filthy beasts deserving of neither honor nor mercy.

A dwarven minstrel, **Faegoor** (Lawful female mountain dwarf expert 4) picks a random character from the crowd and asks him to sing an old dwarven favorite with her. If the character turns in a good performance, the crowd cheers. Otherwise, the fickle guests jeer and mock him for delivering a terrible rendition.

Ingeal Nickelback (Lawful female mountain dwarf expert 5), a quirky yet devout oracle, asks the characters to allow her to bless them after the ceremony. The old dwarf woman places her hands on a character's temples, closes her eyes, and incoherently mumbles. Her strange behavior continues for 1d4 minutes before she suddenly emerges from her self-induced trance and declares that she and the characters share the same dreams. Regardless of the character's denials to the contrary, Ingeal insists that she and the character keep experiencing graphic nightmares of violence, shadows, and triangles in their visions.

Famine

After a few hours of intense eating and hard drinking, the revelers steel their swimming minds and heavy stomachs for the final treat of the evening — tantalizing sweets from the dwarven ovens. The tempting aromas of honey, caramelized sugar, and freshly baked confections dance in the air and on the ravenous diners' tongues. Yet, these magical bouquets mask another far more sinister scent. A character has a 1-in-6 chance to detect a very faint foul sewer stench intertwined with the more pleasant smell. The revelers and servants alike fail to notice the odor or attribute the smell to the ovens in the nearby kitchen.

Sadly, the tasty desserts go to waste as Mirkeer's triad springs their plan into action. As the servants prepare to tote the delicious sweets into the dining hall, the dark folk ignite a large pocket of methane gas located right underneath the thane's feet. The Referee may read or paraphrase the subsequent description of the chaotic scene.

The weary guests brace their stomachs for the final course of the evening, only to be rudely interrupted by what sounds like a peal of thunder and what feels like an earthquake. The ground inexplicably trembles and the ceiling buckles in the wake of a massive explosion. Jagged stone blocks crash to the ground and tumble into a 20-foot-radius crater that instantaneously appears in the center of the floor. These displaced pieces rest on top of the destroyed furniture and mangled bodies beneath them. Agonizing screams and faint whimpers desperately calling for aid are the only sounds heard in the aftermath of the deafening noise that accompanied the ferocious blast.

Dwerfater's most fervent worshippers and can still cast divine magic in his deity's name, but he is a physical wreck. He can barely walk, even with assistance. He cannot pick up a longsword or axe without trembling, and he can hold each weapon only for a few seconds before it falls out of his feeble hands. Kaelan forgets recent events moments after they take place. Nonetheless, Kaelan remains a powerful figure in spite of his limitations. His eyes still sparkle when he speaks of his father Om, his deceased wife Rongara and his children. Now that the characters are official "brothers of the high thane," they have his complete trust. They can converse with him at any time. Throughout the celebration, the characters are free to interact with Kaelan and any of the other guests for as long as the Referee sees fit. The Referee may also use one or more of the following incidents to spice up the party before the dark folk's rude intrusion.

Eara's young, beautiful wife **Arliss** (Neutral female mountain dwarf aristocrat 3) places one arm around a male character's waist. Her breath smells like ale, and she has trouble keeping her balance. The character subjected to this unwanted attention draws glares from Eara. The noble dwarf observes the spectacle for a few moments before reacting to Arliss' flirtation. If the character rebuffs her overtures, Eara sheepishly apologizes to the character before he grabs Arliss and leads her away. A character enamored by Arliss' attention gets a much-different response: Eara confronts the character and accuses him of making advances toward his wife. The loud and unpleasant disturbance instantly alerts Thron to potential trouble. He intercedes and directs an agitated Eara to take the obviously drunk Arliss back to her quarters until she sobers up 1d4 hours later.

Two dwarven soldiers, **Vaalgar** (Neutral male mountain dwarf fighter 4) and **Cirral** (Neutral male mountain dwarf fighter 4), who originally escorted the characters into the banquet hall, conspicuously discuss their heroism in battle. Vaalgar brags that he stood at the vanguard sixty years ago when his unit singlehandedly pushed the hobgoblin battalion back to the walls of Exor. Cirral responds by boasting that he led a furious dwarven charge against a horde of orcs attempting to wrest the Southern Pass from the clan's control. He then mentions his role in fighting off the dark demons and monsters that dwelt below the citadel. The pair is grossly exaggerating most aspects of these conflicts. However, Cirral actually was

Fortunately for the guests, the dwarves' engineering and architectural prowess proves more formidable than the dark folk's nasty surprise. In a fortuitous stroke of luck for the dwarves, the blast originated beneath a section of floor that contained several extremely sturdy tables that absorbed some of the explosion's immense energy. Still, the detonation's effects are devastating. Everyone in the chamber, including the characters and the high thane, has a 60% chance of being struck by debris from the partially collapsed ceiling. These individuals take 6d6 points of damage, or half that amount if they make a saving throw. Whether the save is successful or not, the individual is buried.

In addition, there is a 20% chance that the person was standing or seated in the area now encompassed by the crater. Characters in this area fall 20ft into the hole and take 2d6 points of falling damage. The powerful detonation also caused the underground chamber's walls and ceiling to collapse as well, filling it with additional debris. To make matters worse, some of the coal deposits imbedded in the rocks catch fire after the detonation, filling the air with black smoke. Characters that do not climb out of the crater take 1d6 points of fire damage every round that they spend within the crater. In addition, black smoke fills the air, making it extremely difficult to see and breathe within the fissure. It is possible to

Blassian

Garnock's son already knows what everyone suspects. Trying to appear as unprepared as possible, the outwardly helpful dwarf dashes to the banquet hall unarmed and half-dressed. Blassian is very handsome, with chiseled facial features, a neatly trimmed reddish-brown beard and moustache, braided hair, chilling gray eyes, and a granite jaw. His physique is the exact opposite of the quintessential barrel-chested, stocky dwarf.

Blassian's true intent is to assess the damage and then determine his next step. Like his divine patron, Mirkeer's servant wants to remain in the shadows and not attract unwanted attention. He feigns genuine concern for the victims and rushes from one injured person to another, gauging the severity of their injuries. If he encounters an unconscious or otherwise helpless member of the royal family, the sly Blassian cannot resist the opportunity to eliminate another competitor. He discreetly pours a dose of poisonous powder down the victim's throat. If a character confronts Blassian about his actions, absent any concrete physical evidence, such as an empty vial of the poison, High Thane Kaelan and his heirs do not give any credence to the observer's accusations.

Blassian, Male Mountain Dwarf (Ftr2/Thf6): HD 33; **AC** 4[15]; **Atk** +1 short sword (1d6+1), sling (1d4); **Move** 9; **Save** 9 (+1, ring); **AL** C; **CL/XP** 8/800; **Special:** +2 save bonus vs. traps and magical devices, +4 saves vs. magic, backstab (x3), darkvision 60ft., read languages, thieving skills.

Thieving Skills: Climb 90%, Tasks/Traps 50%, Hear 4 in 6, Hide 40%, Silent 50%, Locks 40%.

Equipment: +2 leather armor, +1 short sword, dagger, sling, 50 sling stones, ring of protection +1, potion of invisibility, 4 doses poison, thieves' tools.

enter the subterranean tunnels through this entry point if the characters extinguish the flames and then remove the 1040 tons of debris that now fills **Area D18** (see **Part II**) and separates them from the now-blocked corridor into the dark folk's lair.

It is impossible to adjudicate what happens to everyone in the banquet hall at the time of the explosion. Of the twelve servants in the room, the falling debris instantly kills seven of them, and two more perish in the slide zone. Likewise, Kaelan and his family suffer a similar fate. The explosion slays two of his four grandsons, one of his brothers, nearly all of his granddaughters, nieces, and respective in-laws. (The Referee may use any means to determine who perishes in the disaster.) Soldiers stationed throughout the high thane's palace arrive on the scene moments later. They frantically remove the stones trapping many of the survivors and scramble to aid their badly injured high thane as well as the characters, if they are in need of rescuing. Dwerfater's clerics also rush to the scene and deploy their magic to heal those wounded in the blast.

Surprisingly, High Thane Kaelan regains his senses remarkably quickly under the circumstances and intently listens to the reports and advice that his surviving family members provide him. The blast's tremendous concussive force seemingly jars him out of his lethargic state and focuses his often-distracted mind on the task at hand. While everyone around him tries to figure out what just happened and why, the suddenly rejuvenated high thane utters two simple words, "dark folk." Despite the surrounding chaos, an eerie silence comes over the frantic chamber with that utterance. Worried facial expressions instantly replace the dogged determination etched onto the survivors' and rescuers' countenances. Sensing the people's distress, the concerned high thane immediately convenes a meeting behind closed doors to discuss the clan's response to the brazen attack.

Into the Breach

As the newest brothers of the high thane, the eyes of Kaelan and his family naturally turn to the characters for aid in these desperate times, even though a few hushed whispers suggest that the characters are willing conspirators in a plot to usurp the high thane and rule in his stead. The isolated handful of doubters is not enough to stem the overwhelming opinion that Clan Craenog needs the adventurers' services more than ever. Despite his fragile emotional and physical state, Kaelan summons his surviving relatives and the characters to a hastily arranged meeting to address the dark folk threat.

From the beginning, High Thane Kaelan insists that the dark folk are responsible for this atrocity, and that this act is merely their opening salvo in a much-greater plan. The high thane and his remaining family unanimously agree that a crushing and immediate response is needed to prevent more bloodshed and further damage to the citadel. If the characters challenge Kaelan's assertion, the energized high thane tenuously rises from his chair, pounds his fist on the table and exclaims, "I was there, thirty-three years ago!" The angry high thane then demands that the characters "behave like true 'brothers of the high thane' and carry out this vital mission, instead of disputing what everyone knows to be true." Kaelan calms down shortly after this outburst and asks the adventurers to delve into the abandoned tunnels beneath the citadel and eradicate the dark folk threat. He tells the characters that they may keep any treasures they discover in underground passageways, including any precious metals that they find. The high thane and his associates reveal the following information to the characters during the course of their discussions.

• Erod Flan rests atop an old quartz mine that they abandoned decades earlier. Still, the dwarves patrolled the dormant tunnels for many years without incident until one of the walls in the main passageway inexplicably collapsed thirty-three years ago. The first engineers sent to investigate the cause disappeared and never returned.

• Kaelan sent a squadron of twenty soldiers to locate the missing dwarves. As they tracked the engineers' movements in the mine, a sizable force of dark folk leapt from their hiding spots and attacked the unit. Only four of the dwarves escaped the onslaught.

• A few days later, 200 dwarven soldiers poured into the subterranean tunnels and confronted the dark folk in a series of bloody engagements. The dwarves outnumbered the dark folk, but their numerical superiority and heavy armor worked against them in the twisting, narrow corridors. The devious dark folk trapped expansive areas of their underground domain. Still, the dwarves prevailed after three weeks of heavy fighting.

• Dwarven engineers permanently sealed the entrance, and Dwerfater's clerics cast magical wards to prevent the dark folk from entering Erod Flan. In spite of their efforts, High Thane Kaelan could not shake a nagging feeling that small pockets of the resilient humanoids escaped the carnage and bided their time waiting for an ideal opportunity to strike. He believes that they deliberately chose this moment for a reason.

• The tunnels are now accessible only through a heavily guarded passage underneath the barracks located in the citadel's southeastern quadrant. A team of six guards monitors the entrance on a continual basis. When the dwarves sealed the tunnels, Kaelan and his most-trusted lieutenant built a well-concealed and magically protected secret passage that would allow the high thane and his soldiers to access the abandoned mine in case of an emergency such as this. There are no reports of any unusual activity in the area, making this situation even more puzzling to the wise and experienced thane.

If the characters accept the high thane's request to destroy the dark folk before they act again, one of his sons or grandsons accompanies the characters to the abandoned tunnels, thus beginning **Part II** of the adventure.

Traitor in the Midst

The clever Blassian keeps a close eye on the high thane and the characters. Several minutes after the high thane summons his surviving family members and the characters into a private audience chamber to discuss the crisis, the crafty rogue quietly enters the room. The attendees nonchalantly acknowledge Blassian's presence as he joins the meeting already in progress. To allay the characters' suspicions, Vaalgar, Cirral, and Ingeal from the **Feast** section of the adventure do the same. Blassian intently listens and says nothing until the very end of the meeting. As the characters prepare to depart for the abandoned quartz mine, Blassian rises to his feet and volunteers to guide the characters through the subterranean tunnels. Vaalgar and Cirral also feign that they were about to offer their services as well. However, they defer to their more-accomplished and better-connected counterpart.

Blassian walks a fine line in this situation. He desperately wants to eliminate the meddling characters with the help of his dark folk allies, but he does not want to be overly aggressive and give the impression that he has an ulterior motive. Blassian states his case for joining the expedition by pointing out that he is familiar with the mine and has experience fighting the dark folk, both of which are true statements. He dismisses any attempts to excavate the crater and infiltrate the subterranean complex via this route as utter folly. Blassian passionately explains that the explosion dislodged tons of rock and stone, and even after excavating the debris, any passages granting access to the dark folk's complex may also be in ruins. He states that any time spent chasing this fruitless goblin dog is a waste of valuable resources. Though he obviously prefers to play an active role in the exploration of the tunnels, he does not insist or demand that he accompany the characters on their mission or that they abandon any efforts to confront the dark folk through their proverbial back door. In the end, he acquiesces to the characters' wishes. Blassian's actions are described in detail in **Part II** of the adventure.

Part II: Dark Shadows

After learning of the devastating blast that tore through the high thane's banquet hall, Erod Flan is understandably on edge. It is now up to the characters to calm the citizens' frayed nerves and delve into the underground tunnels to prevent another explosion and neutralize the dark folk's threat once and for all. In the depths below the dwarven capital, the characters soon realize that their enemy spent many years planning for this seminal moment. False entryways, devious traps, ambushes, and murder holes block the characters' passage through the dark folk's sinister lair. Blassian, the treacherous turncoat, also conspires against the characters. He either leads them straight into the dark folk's most lethal obstacle, or he joins their allies and participates in the attack against the daring adventurers. In addition to Blassian, the characters must also battle the dark folk's leader, Rogvörn, as well as his bloody bones intermediary in order to prevail in their quest to save Erod Flan from near-certain destruction. In spite of their success, the characters come to the frightening realization that their road ultimately takes them to the distant citadel of Tyr Whin and a confrontation with Grugdour, the ambitious hobgoblin overlord and his war machine.

Into Darkness

There are two ways into the dark folk's subterranean realm, though neither path is easy. The high thane and his entourage direct the characters to the dwarves' only known entrance into the mines through the guarded passage beneath the southeastern barracks. Entering the underground complex via this route is simply a matter of walking through the secret passage that connects the surface world with the mines. High Thane Kaelan tells the characters where to find the hidden entrance, which comes as a shock to the clan's stunned guards, who had no idea of its existence. With that said, the dark folk expect the dwarves to use this entrance, regardless of whether the current high thane and his heirs perished in the explosion. The dark folk are well prepared for an assault from this direction.

Alternately, the characters can excavate the stones and debris from the crater, extinguish the flames and then gain access to the dark folk's realm in this manner. Unless the characters use magic to pass through the stones or otherwise remove them, it takes a tremendous, concerted effort to clear the rubble from the blocked corridor and enter the dark folk's lair through the proverbial backdoor. In addition to the hard labor needed to move 1040 tons of rock and stone from an 80ft-deep crater, the characters must also overcome the heat and thick, black smoke emitted by the smoldering

Running Blassian

The would-be thane has bided his time for decades, so he has the patience to wait at least a few more days to claim his elusive prize. As mentioned in **Part I** of the adventure, Blassian prefers to accompany the characters into the quartz mine. Thanks to Mirkeer's intercession, the traitorous dwarf is aware of the numerous traps that lie in wait for unsuspecting characters as they pass through the quartz mine. If the characters allow Blassian to lead or guide them through the underground complex, he deliberately takes them to a trapped intersection (**Area Q4A**) and tips them off to the trap's presence as a means of further gaining their trust. Later, he takes the characters out of their way to encounter the traps in **Area Q4B** and **Area Q4C**. Likewise, Blassian also fights to the best of his abilities against the mindless livestones inhabiting **Area Q4**, yet he fights defensively against the fungus lichenthropes. He never backstabs either of the preceding foes.

Blassian considers the grimlocks to be his strongest allies. If the cunning monstrous humanoids surprise the characters or act before the characters during the initial round of contact, the treacherous dwarf flies into a rage and backstabs the most vulnerable character, preferably a magic-user. If the tide of battle turns against Blassian and his grimlock allies, he discreetly quaffs his *potion of invisibility* and tries to escape unnoticed. In this case, Blassian heads back toward the mine's entrance and attempts to convince the high thane and his court that the characters ambushed him in the quartz mines. Despite Blassian's bluff, Kaelan expresses skepticism about his distant relative's odd story. In spite of his cloudy memory, the aging high thane quickly points out that Blassian volunteered his services to the expedition. If the characters intended to kill his traitorous cousin from the beginning, the high thane surmises that the characters would have

sought out Blassian and made sure that he accompanied them into the mines. Kaelan believes Blassian is too ashamed to admit his cowardice in battle and instead concocted this elaborate ruse to conceal the truth. He dismisses his cousin's ridiculous charges and awaits word from the characters before committing more troops to the mines. The high thane and his family discreetly confine Blassian to his quarters until the immediate crisis subsides. Fearful of losing his bid to succeed Kaelan, the scheming dwarf reluctantly complies.

If the characters refused Blassian's services, the conniving rogue cajoles the guards in **Area Q1** to allow him to pass and explore the tunnels on his own. He then monitors the characters' progress in the quartz mine. Once they come into contact with the grimlocks or if one of the traps deals significant damage to the characters, Blassian attacks as described in the preceding section. In the event that the characters avoided the grimlocks, Blassian instead attacks the characters when they encounter one of the dark stalkers in either **Area D3** or **Area D6**.

Despite his lofty political ambitions, self-preservation is first and foremost on Blassian's mind. Blassian surrenders if reduced to fewer than 10 hit points. If the characters successfully intimidate their untrustworthy kin or magically compel him to speak against his will, Blassian reveals that he is merely a pawn in a grander plan. He tells the characters that the dark folk are a distraction, and that the real danger lies farther north at the remote outpost of Tyr Whin where Grugdour, the new hobgoblin overlord, and his army of thousands of troops are moving into position to attack the venerable dwarven fortress. Blassian also confesses that his first act as high thane would be to transfer 500 troops from Tyr Whin to Erod Flan to deliberately leave Tyr Whin more vulnerable to the hobgoblins' attack under the guise of protecting the capital.

coal deposits. Furthermore, the process of manually removing the heavy objects from the explosion site creates tremendous noise that alerts the dark folk to the characters' presence.

Once the characters decide upon their route, the adventure proceeds to the appropriate locale on the accompanying map of the dark folk's realm. If the characters go through the entrance below the southeastern barracks, the adventure begins at **Area Q1**. Characters that opt to excavate the crater instead of using the secret passage start their exploration in **Area D18**.

Quartz Mine Features

The dwarves constructed the quartz mine for functionality rather than aesthetics. There are no unstable or structurally unsound areas within the mine. All surfaces are carved out of rough-hewn stone and the average ceiling height is 2d3+2ft. There are no doors on this level. The dwarves have darkvision, therefore, there are no light sources throughout the complex.

Q1. Barracks Passageway

> Stone stairs descend at a steep angle into a nondescript, rough-hewn stone corridor. Six dwarves clad in half-plate armor stand at attention against the walls. They carry dwarven waraxes and light crossbows. Massive stones fused together with mortar block the remainder of the passageway.

In spite of their attentiveness, the **6 dwarven soldiers** (Neutral male mountain dwarf fighter 3) defending the entrance into the quartz mine are jittery and concerned. They are part of a rotation of 24 soldiers assigned to this duty, and they insist that neither they nor any of their counterparts heard or saw anything unusual up to, during, and after the explosion. The stone and mortar barrier separating **Area Q1** from **Area Q3** also holds a few unexpected surprises. The dwarves inlaid a thin sheet of lead roughly midway through the obstacle as well as other alloys to foil divination spells and attempts to bypass the barrier by manipulating the stone.

The dwarves manning this entrance are stunned to learn of the secret passage that grants access to the other side of the corridor. The characters are aware of the portal's existence and location. It may take several tries, but the characters eventually find the secret door.

Q2. Secret Passage

> A rough-hewn, stone corridor turns west and disappears behind the bend.
> The secret passage simultaneously serves as an access point for the dwarves to enter the mine and a formidable deterrent to other creatures attempting to infiltrate Erod Flan from below the citadel. The dwarves placed a powerful **trap** at the section of corridor bearing the "**T**" symbol. The magical trap does no harm to dwarves, but it releases a deafening blast of sonic energy whenever anything else steps across it. Any characters within 5ft of the blast takes 4d8 points of damage unless they make a saving throw for half damage. The high thane is aware of the spell's triggering condition, and he gives the password to a halfling or another race with strong ties to the dwarves. He conveniently "forgets" the triggering condition for all others.

A *wizard lock* (caster level 6) protects the **secret door** on the opposite side of the corridor. The locking mechanism can be found on the side of the door facing **Area Q2**, thus allowing the dwarves to use the lock to enter into **Area Q3** rather than vice versa.

Q3. Mine Entrance

The rough-hewn stone corridor turns west and splits into two narrower passages.

> Before Bretton Chiselear, Erod Flan's legendary cleric of Dwerfater, left this world to spend eternity with his divine patron, he performed one last service for his people. He cast a potent *symbol of death* on the portal connecting **Area Q2** and **Area Q3**. The symbol triggers whenever any non-dwarf passes through the portal, so once again a non-dwarf character must figure out a way to circumvent triggering the lethal spell. As in **Area Q2**, the high thane may provide the password to a non-dwarf based upon the circumstances. Once triggered, the symbol becomes inactive for 10 minutes before it can be triggered again. Needless to say, Bretton's powerful magic served its purpose, keeping the dark folk at bay and forcing them to devise an alternate means of avenging their defeat.

Q4. Mine Shafts

> Narrow, twisting corridors bore deeper into the earth at a slight, yet noticeable angle. The rough-hewn stone passageways show visible signs of tunneling and excavating and are also covered by thick layers of mold, lichens, and fungi.

The adjoining mine shafts and tunnels are narrower and less precise than the rough-hewn corridor that connects the subterranean complex with the surface world. The passageways generally descend between 10 and 20 degrees into the ground. The dark folk spent the better part of this decade preparing for their potential rematch against their dwarven adversaries. They cleverly populated the mineshafts with guardians that are immune to the numerous traps scattered throughout the complex. There are three different groups of creatures that roam the mineshafts.

Lichenthropes

The most numerous are the 18 lichenthropes that tend to the plant growth coating the mineshafts' surface areas. The alien creatures wander the passages in groups of six. There is a 40% chance of encountering one of their patrols for every 10 minutes spent wandering through Area Q4.

Lichenthropes (6): HD 3; **HP** 23, 21x2, 19, 18, 15; **AC** 6[13]; **Atk** bite (1d6); **Move** 12; **Save** 12; **AL** C; **CL/XP** 5/240; **Special:** contagion (target takes 50% damage, begins transformation into lichenthrope over 1d4 weeks, 50% chance of turning into patch of fungus), magic resistance (25%, hound form only), shapechange (humanoid or hound). (**Monstrosities** 295)

Tactics: The dark folk responsible for the lichenthropes' creation now exert nominal control over the creatures. The **6 lichenthropes** wade into melee combat, attempting to encircle the characters and attack them with their bite. The lichenthropes do not retreat and never surrender.

Treasure: The strange creatures never stray more than 10d10 x 10ft from their permanent lair. The lichenthropes always bury their worldly goods beneath a small pile of fungus. The treasure consists of 6d6 agate stones worth 10gp each and 2d6 garnets worth 100gp each.

Livestone

The 3 livestones that inhabit these tunnels are long-time residents of the dwarven mines. These strange oozes are solitary predators that lie in wait for potential prey to wander too close to their lair. There is a 30% chance of encountering a livestone for every 10 minutes spent in Area Q4. It takes a successful DC 18 Perception check to spot the concealed creature while moving past it. When the characters encounter one of the three livestones, the Referee may read or paraphrase the following description.

A slab of moss-covered stone separates from the surrounding rock and transforms into a grayish ooze that forms a solidified pseudopod.

The livestone slams into its prey and then attempts to engulf its hapless opponent. The mindless creature has no concept of strategy or death, so it uses this tactic until it slays its target or the characters kill it. The unintelligent ooze has no treasure.

Livestones (3): HD 5; HP 36, 35x2; AC 9[10]; Atk slam (1d8); Move 9; Save 12; AL C; CL/XP 7/600; Special: engulf (1 hp damage per round, save avoids), immunity to petrification, solidify (8d6 damage to engulfed targets unless save for half), surprise (1–4 on 1d6). (**The Tome of Horrors Complete** 361)

Grimlocks

The dark folk are not alone in hating the dwarves. There is a 20% chance of encountering 4 grimlocks for every ten minutes spent exploring Area Q4. The monstrous humanoids are born hunters who sneak up on their prey and slice their foes into pieces.

Grimlocks (4): HD 4; HP 28, 26, 25x2; AC 4[15]; Atk battle axe (1d8); Move 12; Save 13; AL C; CL/XP 5/240; Special: immune to gaze attacks, illusions and visual effects. (**Tome of Horrors 4** 116)
    Equipment: tattered hides, stone axe, pouch containing 2d6 pieces of quartz worth 10gp each. One of the grimlocks also wears a helm of reading magic and languages.

Tactics: The grimlocks fly into a wild rage the instant they detect a dwarf. Their tactics are simple: Whenever possible, they use their knowledge of the terrain to surround their enemies and eviscerate them with blinding efficiency. They continue hacking at their foes until one side falls in battle. Surrender and retreat are not in their vocabulary.

Q4A. Stand or Fall

The dark folk positioned this devious pitfall trap at four strategically positioned locations within the tunnels. Unlike most lethal devices, this clever booby trap has two separate components that work in unison. The first part is a hold person trap that affects dwarves and other humanoids, but has no effect against the lichenthropes, livestones, and grimlocks. The trap triggers whenever a humanoid steps into the area. The creature must make a saving throw with a –2 penalty or be held immobile for 1d4+2 rounds. The trap affects only the first creature to activate it.

The device's second and far-more-lethal component is the **deadfall trap** beneath the creature. It takes the floor approximately 3 seconds to split apart and open into a 120ft-deep pit with sheer vertical walls. In fact, the floor separates so slowly that any creature not paralyzed or held can easily step aside to avoid falling into the chasm. A paralyzed creature is not as fortunate. Unless another character can take an immediate action to rescue the held humanoid, that creature falls to the bottom and takes 12d6 points of falling damage. The trapped passage of the floor returns to its normal position 1 minute after activating the trap.

Q4B. Demonic Dreams

In comparison to the preceding trap, the dark folk's next trick is much simpler yet equally deadly. The sly creatures engraved 3 symbol traps throughout the complex. Whenever a dwarf steps over an area protected by one of these potent spells, a shadow demon is instantly summoned to the location. It immediately attacks the offending creature and its allies for the next 12 rounds, or until the characters destroy it, whichever comes first.

Shadow Demon: HD 7; AC 4[15]; Atk 2 claws (1d6), bite (1d8); Move 15 (fly); Save 9; AL C; CL/XP 12/2000; Special: immunities (electricity, poison), incorporeal, shadow blend (surprise, 1–5 on 1d6), spell-like abilities, sunlight powerless, telepathy 100ft. (**The Tome of Horrors Complete** 151)
    Spell-like abilities: at will—darkness 15ft radius; 3/day—fear; 1/week—magic jar.

Q4C. Dark Folk Say

Alien artwork depicting humanoid figures covered in thick linens decapitating and torturing dwarves covers the walls. Hand-shaped indentations are scattered among the crude paintings.

Like the preceding traps, this sinister barrier has two components. The first part is a **suggestion trap** uttered in dwarven that directs the individuals to place their hands atop the impressions built into the wall surfaces. The trap's first component triggers whenever a humanoid approaches within 10ft of the corridor's end. Creatures within 30ft of the trap that can understand dwarven when it is triggered must make a saving throw or follow the suggestion.

True to form, the second part of the trap emulates what the characters see in the artwork. As soon as the character places one of their hands inside of the impression, a **concealed blade** springs from the wall and attempts to lop off the unfortunate creature's head. The trap is constructed specifically for dwarves, i.e. the blade strikes an area where a dwarf's head would normally be. The blade does 2d4 points of damage to anyone it hits. If the target is a dwarf or halfling (or someone of similar size), the blade also has a 20% chance of beheading the target.

Q5. Passageway

The dark, rough-hewn corridor heads west before making an abrupt turn toward the southeast. The passageway continues in that direction for as far as the eye can see.

A secret door once separated this passageway leading into the dark folk's lair from the dwarves' quartz mine. The dark folk dismantled the door after the dwarves' departure from the quartz mine. The passageway continues heading in a south-southeasterly direction for approximately 300ft before reaching the final obstacle in reaching the dark folk's complex — a narrow, twisting tunnel embedded with razor-sharp pieces of jagged obsidian. The passageway descends into the earth at a 30-degree angle. To make matters worse, the humanoids applied a thin layer of grease onto the smooth surface, making it extremely difficult to negotiate the descent without falling and potentially sliding to the bottom of the tunnel. The Referee may read or paraphrase the following description of this sinister barrier.

An oily substance glistens on the smooth surface of a polished, stone tunnel that twists and turns at sharp angles all while descending deeper below the surface at a 30-degree angle. Shards of volcanic glass protrude from the walls, floor and ceiling. The subterranean passageway is barely wide and tall enough to accommodate a dwarf-sized creature.

In order to avoid coming into contact with the keen edges of the volcanic glass, a dwarf-sized character moving at half his normal speed must roll below his dexterity on 3d6 to avoid the dangerous obstacles and not fall prone. Only one check is needed each round. A character can move at full speed, but must roll on 4d6 against his dexterity. Characters larger than dwarves must always roll on 4d6 against their dexterity to avoid coming into contact with the embedded obsidian while moving through the tunnel. Creatures larger than humans cannot squeeze through the tunnel at all.

Each time that a character fails a check, he takes 1d6 points of slashing damage from the embedded glass. Worse still, the character also falls prone and slides down the tunnel for 1d3 x 10ft, taking an additional 1d4 points of slashing damage for every 10ft traveled in this manner.

Removing the embedded obsidian is a slow, laborious task. It takes one creature 20 minutes to safely clear out a 10ft section of the tunnel. Two creatures can complete the task in half the time. However, it is impossible to fit more than two creatures in any 10ft section of the tunnel.

After negotiating passage through the obsidian tunnel, the subterranean artery widens and returns to its previous state as a rough-hewn stone corridor. After proceeding for another 250ft, the passageway ends at **Area D1**, one of the entrances into the dark folk's lair.

Ad Hoc XP Award: The Referee may award characters 3200 XP to characters that successfully negotiate the obsidian passageway without taking any damage. An award of 1600 XP is appropriate for adventuring parties that take damage from the obstacle.

Dark Folk Complex Features

The dark folk's ancestral home predates the dwarves' quartz mine by at least several hundred years. If not for the dark folk's exploratory tunnel burrowing into the dwarves' quartz mine, the two races may have never come into contact. Unlike their dwarven adversaries, the chaotic humanoids are not master stonemasons or architects. Still, there are no unstable or structurally unsound areas. However, pockets of methane gas pose a much-greater and less-predictable danger to the characters. There is a 10% chance of encountering this hazard for every 10 minutes spent in the area.

Methane

This highly volatile gas is typically encountered deep underground or in areas with large concentrations of coal. Methane is colorless, and unfortunately for subterranean explorers, it is odorless. The typical pocket of methane has a radius of 1d6 x 10ft. Any exposure to an open flame or spark causes an explosion for 6d6 points of damage (saving throw for half) to all within the radius of the gas plus an additional 1d6 x 20ft beyond the original radius. Many miners use canaries or other sentinel animals to detect the gas before they hit a pocket and risk an explosion.

T. Dark Folk Traps

In addition to the natural hazards prevalent throughout the dark folk's complex, the cunning humanoids also tailor made several traps specifically designed to ensnare their dwarven adversaries. All of these traps operate with pressure plates that are activated whenever a creature weighing 150 pounds or greater steps onto the trapped section of floor. These areas are denoted by a "T" that appears on the accompanying map of the dark folk's lair. Presented below are three traps that the Referee may choose or randomly select to challenge the characters during their exploration of the complex.

Black Smear Trap

Bolts coated with black smear poison target all creatures within 10ft. The bolts strike as a 4HD creature and do 1d4 points of damage. Any creature struck must make a saving throw or lose 1d2 points of strength for 2d6–1 rounds. Any creature whose strength falls to 0 dies.

Falling Stones Trap

Heavy blocks of stone fall, crushing all creatures in a 10ft area unless they make a saving throw to dodge out of the way. Any creature struck takes 6d6 points of damage and has a 75% chance of being pinned beneath the stones.

Floor Trap with Yellow Mold

A 30ft-deep pit opens below all characters in a 10ft line. Anyone who fails a saving throw to jump clear falls 30ft into a patch of **yellow mold**.

Yellow Mold: HD n/a; AC n/a; Atk 1d6 damage plus spore cloud; **Move** 0; **Save** n/a; **AL** N; **CL/XP** 3/60; **Special**: killed by fire, poisonous spore cloud (10ft diameter, save or die). (**Monstrosities** 336)

All surfaces are carved out of rough-hewn stone and the average ceiling height is 2d3+2ft. The dark folk manufactured their doors from an unusual hardened fungus that has the same statistics as a good wooden door. The dark folk can see in darkness, thus there are no light sources anywhere in the complex unless otherwise specified.

The dark folk are supremely confident that their assortment of traps and guardians is sufficient to deter adventurers from pressing the fight to them. With the traitorous Blassian presumably in charge of Clan Craenog, they expect him to send his fellow dwarves to their deaths in the trapped quartz mine and then sue for peace. They do not expect adventurers to reach their lair either through the quartz mine or by excavating the crater. Still, the malevolent humanoids keep a wary eye toward both entry points, but they are not fully mobilized or on high alert for intruders.

D1. Antechamber

Thin strips of fungi partially cover crude and gruesome sculptures of unbridled savagery that adorn the walls. Unlike the walls, the floor's surface hosts several much-larger species of brown, gray and purple mushrooms and fungi.

The dark folk's art is primitive and violent. Graphic wall sculptures depict the small humanoids eviscerating scores of dwarves as well as an assortment of other common, subterranean races such as the drow and troglodytes. Like these races, the dark folk make ample use of the indigenous plant life to feed their population and guard it. Interspersed among the ordinary fungi species are **4 violet fungi**. The violet fungi immediately attack intruders entering the chamber from **Area Q5**. In addition, **2 shriekers** also share the room with the smaller plants. Unlike the violet fungi, these two, man-sized plants do not engage the characters in combat. As the name suggests, the mindless plants loose a piercing sound as soon as the violet fungi respond to the characters. The deafening noise lasts for 1d3 rounds and attracts the interest of the occupants of **Area D2** who come to investigate the cacophony.

Violet Fungi (4): HD 3; HP 22, 20, 17, 15; AC 7[12]; Atk 4 tendrils (rot); **Move** 1; **Save** 14; **AL** N; **CL/XP** 4/120; **Special**: tendrils cause rot (save resists). (**Monstrosities** 183)

Shriekers (2): HD 3; HP 21, 20; AC 7[12]; Atk none; **Move** 1; **Save** 14; **AL** N; **CL/XP** 3/60; **Special**: shriek (30ft radius, 1hp damage per round, save resists). (**Monstrosities** 423)

D2. Antechamber

Three columns carved out of hardened fungus presumably support the nearly eight-foot-high ceiling. A dozen black robes in a range of different sizes hang from fungal protrusions in the columns. A black, leather glove affixed to the front of a door is made from the same substance as the columns.

Inspired by his mystical new deity, Rogvörn experimented with new forms of magic and strange creations. The **2 rag golems** that occupy the antechamber represent his greatest creations. In most likelihood, the creatures answered the shriekers' call from **Area D1** and are no longer here. However, if the characters somehow bypassed the violet fungi and shriekers, these two constructs stand ready to defend the dark folk's adjacent temple. The rag golems instantly attack any creature other than dark folk. Like their creators, the mindless constructs use their ability to conjure magical darkness to their maximum advantage. They surround their foes in impenetrable blackness, which blinds their enemies yet has no effect on them. They repeatedly pommel their adversaries until either party is destroyed.

The black robes hanging from the columns are ceremonial garb that the dark folk must wear at all times while in the adjoining temple. There are 12 robes of various sizes. The characters may don the robes as a disguise to infiltrate the creatures' temple.

Rag Golems (2): HD 6; HP 30x2; AC 7[12]; Atk 2 slams (1d4 plus aura of darkness); **Move** 9; **Save** 14; **AL** N; **CL/XP** 8/800; **Special:** aura of darkness (touch surrounds target with darkness, save or −1 to hit, save or damage), immune to most magic, spell-like ability, vulnerable to fire (200%). (See **Sidebox**)
> **Spell-like ability:** at-will—*darkness 15ft radius*.

The door requires some effort to open, but it is also protected by a **trap** attuned to allow only worshippers of Mirkeer and Hecate to pass through it unharmed. Any other creature trying to open the door causes a fiery burst to explode. The blast hits anyone within a 5ft radius for 3d6 points of damage (saving throw for half).

The black leather glove on the door is the religious symbol of Mirkeer, the daughter of Hecate.

Golem, Rag

Hit Dice: 6 (30 hit points)
Armor Class: 7[12]
Attacks: 2 slams (1d4 plus aura of darkness)
Saving Throw: 11
Special: aura of darkness, *darkness 15ft radius*, spell-like ability,
Move: 9
Alignment: Neutrality
Number Encountered: 1
Challenge Level: 8/800

The faint stench of body odor and offal accompanies a humanoid-shaped mass of soiled, moldy rags propelled by a pair of grotesquely oversized legs created from filthy linens. Rag golems are formed from the castoff belongings of dark creepers or dark stalkers. Any creature struck by a rag golem must make a saving throw or be enveloped in an aura of darkness. The creature takes a −1 penalty to hit, saves and damage for 1 round until the darkness fades. They can cast *darkness 15ft radius* at will. Rag golems are immune to most magic except fire-based spells, which do double damage.

Rag Golem: HD 6 (30 hit points); **AC** 7[12]; **Atk** 2 slams (1d4 plus aura of darkness); **Move** 9; **Save** 14; **AL** N; **CL/XP** 8/800; **Special:** aura of darkness (touch surrounds target with darkness, save or −1 to hit, save or damage), immune to most magic, spell-like ability, vulnerable to fire (200%).
> **Spell-like ability:** at-will—*darkness 15ft radius*.

D3. Temple of Mirkeer

> An impenetrable veil of darkness shields what lies beyond the threshold.

Unlike most temples, Mirkeer's place of worship is entirely undecorated other than a jagged, oval onyx stone that functions as an altar. Normally, Rogvörn leads the congregation in worship. However, he is currently in **Area D17**, where he is busy building another trigger for a secondary explosion.

The activities of Mirkeer's devout worshippers remain hidden behind the *darkness* effect that fills the temple. Fortunately, the **dark stalker** and **6 dark creepers** that occupy the temple are currently practicing the ritual of praying to their shadowy deity while blindfolded. They too are unaware of the characters' presence unless the characters trigger the trap cast upon the threshold or dispel the magical darkness. If Blassian accompanies the characters, he immediately alerts the dark folk and sneak attacks his closest foe. Otherwise, the dark folk remain oblivious to the intrusion until the characters attack them or reveal themselves. Whenever either event occurs, the dark folk charge en mass as they attempt to engulf their enemies in a sea of rags and daggers. The dark folk fight best in magical darkness, so at least one dark creeper or the dark stalker uses their spell-like abilities to keep the area cloaked in pitch blackness. The dwarves' hated rivals fight to the bitter end and never surrender, especially in the virtual presence of their revered goddess.

Dark Creepers (6): HD 1+1; HP 9, 8, 7x2, 6, 5; AC 7[12] or 0[19] in darkness; Atk dagger (1d4 plus poison); **Move** 9; **Save** 17; **AL** C; **CL/XP** 3/60; **Special:** backstab (x2), create special darkness (50ft radius, 1/day, extinguish normal light sources, magical light sources save or extinguished, darkvision fails), death-flash (10ft radius, save or blinded for 1d6 rounds), level 4 thief. (*Monstrosities* 83)
> **Thieving Skills:** Climb 88%, Tasks/Traps 30%, Hear 4 in 6, Hide 25%, Silent 35%, Locks 25%.
> **Equipment:** dagger, 3 doses of black smear poison (save or lose 1d2 strength for 2d6−1 rounds, death at 0 strength).

Dark Stalker: HD 6+2; HP 43; AC 7[12] or 0[19] in darkness; Atk short sword (1d6 plus poison); **Move** 12; **Save** 11; **AL** C; **CL/XP** 8/800; **Special:** backstab (x2), create special darkness (50ft radius, 3/day, extinguish normal light sources, magical light sources save or extinguished, darkvision fails), death-flash (40ft radius, save or 3d6 damage), level 4 thief. (*Monstrosities* 84)
> **Thieving Skills:** Climb 88%, Tasks/Traps 30%, Hear 4 in 6, Hide 25%, Silent 35%, Locks 25%.
> **Equipment:** leather armor, 2 short swords, 6 doses of black smear poison (save or lose 1d2 strength for 2d6−1 rounds, death at 0 strength), *potion of extra healing*, *potion of heroism*, pouch with 2 emeralds (500gp each).

Treasure: The dark creepers carry a total of 42 agate stones worth 10 gp each and 97gp.

D4. Rogvörn's Chamber

> An oddly shaped stone with a removable lid occupies the floor several feet away from a pile of ragged, unevenly dispersed linens that apparently functions as a bed. A mound of fungi roughly shaped into the likeness of a storage jar is against the near wall. A flat piece of hardened, green material serves as a crude lid.

Rogvörn serves as the dark folk's de facto high priest even though he can cast only a handful of divine spells. The tribe's leader normally sleeps in this chamber, but in light of recent events, he moved to a more secure location for at least the time being. In spite of his safety concerns, Rogvörn still stores his treasures and important documents in his personal quarters. He irrationally fears losing his precious items to would-be thieves from among his kin, so he safeguards them with traps designed to be more annoying rather than destructive.

The stone "chest" is an ideal example of this principle. The 3ft-diameter, 1ft-high stone resembles a wide, conventional cooking pot with a lid. Rogvörn keeps his monetary treasures inside the secure vessel. The lid features a small handle that facilitates opening the stone with ease. Rogvörn coated the handle with a fast-acting adhesive. The substance instantly bonds to any object or creature that contacts it. The adhesive permanently affixes the handle to any non-organic matter. In comparison, the bond dissolves 4d6 hours after coming into physical contact with living tissue. The lid is 3ft in diameter and weighs 50 lbs., though it can be broken into smaller pieces to make it more manageable. Still, having a piece of stone attached to one's hand makes it impossible to hold an object in that hand and also imposes a 20% chance of spell failure. The lid can be safely removed by lifting it along its edges or merely sliding it off the top without coming into contact with the handle.

The specially grown fungus against the opposite wall is shaped into the likeness of an ancient amphora without the trademark handles. It also has a hinged fungus flap atop the opening. The dark caller stores personal documents inside this container. Unlike the preceding mechanism, the fungus container is a **conventional trap**. Flipping open the lid releases a cloud of toxic gas. Any creature within a 5ft radius breathing the burnt othur fumes must make a saving throw or begin choking for 1d6 points of damage per round.

The fungus quickly repairs any damage within 1d4 minutes, so Rogvörn bypasses the trap by passing his hand through the soft, malleable plant matter without releasing any of the lethal poison. At the present time, the fungus amphora contains a map of the Stoneheart Mountain region stretching from Erod Flan to the south to the hobgoblin citadels and Tyr Whin much farther north. The map features an arrow pointing from Exor to Tyr Whin, and a notation written in dark folk that reads, "*Grugdour.*" If the characters gathered rumors about the Stoneheart Mountains in **Part I** of the adventure, they may already be familiar with the name of Exor's hobgoblin commander.

Rogvörn uses the mass of soiled linens as a crude bed. It contains nothing of significance.

Treasure: Inside of the stone chest are 1488gp as well as 4 black pearls worth 500gp each and a *wand of mirror image* (3 charges).

D5. Guard Room

Two large toadstool mushrooms with gnawed caps literally sprout from the filthy floor coated in a thin layer of dirt and slime. Four mounds of moldy linens cover the remainder of the floor.

The **6 dark creepers** stationed in this guard room feast on the squat, dwarf-sized mushroom caps to break up the monotony. Without the direction of their dark stalker and dark caller masters, the dark creepers are somewhat lackadaisical considering the circumstances. Unless they are alerted to the presence of intruders outside of the door, they are lying down on the filthy rags. Nevertheless, the dark creepers still rally in defense of their subterranean home and fight the intruders to the bitter end.

Dark Creepers (6): HD 1+1; **HP** 9x2, 8x2, 7, 6; **AC** 7[12] or 0[19] in darkness; **Atk** dagger (1d4 plus poison); **Move** 9; **Save** 17; **AL** C; **CL/XP** 3/60; **Special:** backstab (x2), create special darkness (50ft radius, 1/day, extinguish normal light sources, magical light sources save or extinguished, darkvision fails), death-flash (10ft radius, save or blinded for 1d6 rounds), level 4 thief. (**Monstrosities** 83)
    Thieving Skills: Climb 88%, Tasks/Traps 30%, Hear 4 in 6, Hide 25%, Silent 35%, Locks 25%.

Equipment: dagger, 3 doses of black smear poison (save or lose 1d2 strength for 2d6–1 rounds, death at 0 strength).

Treasure: The dark creepers carry their listed gear as well as 6 garnets worth 100gp each.

D6. Prison

Hardened fungal bars wall off a section of the far wall and form a rudimentary prison. A badly malnourished and physically abused middle-aged dwarf lies in a pool of his own filth inside a cramped cell. Four stone chairs surround a solidified mushroom cap that functions as a table. A stone column with built-in manacles is against the near wall.

The dwarf prisoner is not alone in this chamber. His jailor is a sadistic and malevolent **dark stalker** named Ragnarn. The cruel overseer and his **3 dark creeper** servants relentlessly torment their subject. Unlike typical humanoid prisons, the fungal door is kept unlocked, though it is still stuck like the other portals in this complex. The characters' intrusion immediately springs the quartet into action. Ragnarn uses his darkness ability to plunge the area into magical blackness and then uses the prevailing lighting conditions to backstab his adversaries. The dark creepers fight to the death and only speak if forced to do so. The dark creepers know nothing of significance. However, Ragnarn is aware that their divine patron forged an alliance between the dark folk, a traitorous dwarf, and the hobgoblins in the north, who imminently intend to assault Tyr Whin.

Ragnarn, Dark Stalker: HD 6+2; **HP** 43; **AC** 7[12] or 0[19] in darkness; **Atk** +1 short sword (1d6+1 plus poison), sling (1d4); **Move** 12; **Save** 10 (+1, cloak); **AL** C; **CL/XP** 8/800; **Special:** backstab (x3), create special darkness (50ft radius, 3/day, extinguish normal light sources, magical light sources save or extinguished, darkvision fails), death-flash (40ft radius, save or 3d6 damage), level 6 thief. (**Monstrosities** 84)
    Thieving Skills: Climb 90%, Tasks/Traps 40%, Hear 4 in 6, Hide 35%, Silent 45%, Locks 35%.
    Equipment: leather armor, 2 +1 short swords, sling, 20 sling stones, *cloak of protection +1*, 6 doses of black smear poison (save or lose 1d2 strength for 2d6–1 rounds, death at 0 strength), *potion of extra healing*.

Dark Creepers (3): HD 1+1; **HP** 8, 6x2; **AC** 7[12] or 0[19] in darkness; **Atk** dagger (1d4 plus poison); **Move** 9; **Save** 17; **AL** C; **CL/XP** 3/60; **Special:** create special darkness (50ft radius, 1/day, extinguish normal light sources, magical light sources save or extinguished, darkvision fails), death-flash (10ft radius, save or blinded for 1d6 rounds), level 4 thief. (**Monstrosities** 83)
    Thieving Skills: Climb 88%, Tasks/Traps 30%, Hear 4 in 6, Hide 25%, Silent 35%, Locks 25%.
    Equipment: dagger, 3 doses of black smear poison (save or lose 1d2 strength for 2d6–1 rounds, death at 0 strength).

Development: The dark folk captured their unfortunate prisoner, **Doel Thumbcracker** (Neutral male mountain dwarf fighter 3) during the dwarves' last raid into their lair more than 30 years ago. Three decades of abuse and despair took their toll on his jovial demeanor and optimistic personality. Still, the sight of his kin and the prospect of freedom buoy his sagging spirits. The dark folk tortured him on and off for the better part of his stay. At first, they demanded information about Erod Flan, yet their attention recently shifted away from Clan Craenog's capital and pointed in the direction of Tyr Whin. He also notes that the dark folk started asking him about a group of adventurers, i.e. the characters, just a few weeks earlier. He does not think that the dark folk are planning to attack the distant fortress themselves. Instead, he believes that they are gathering information for someone else.

There is no conventional door that allows access into Doel's cell. The fungal bars must be broken down and his manacles must be removed to free him.

D7. Communal Chamber

The fetid air bombards the senses. In spite of the 12-foot-high ceilings and ample ventilation, the foul odors of sweat and offal still fill the air. Nine misshapen mushroom caps roughly equivalent to the size of a large tent spread throughout the cavernous chamber. The hardened fungi are almost completely carved out like a jack-o'-lantern (sans the eyes) with a small, oval opening serving as the crude abode's entrance. Piles of festering rags and linens litter the floor of these cramped residences.

The resident dark creepers dwell in abject squalor within these disgusting homes. They sometimes cram up to six small humanoids within these tiny, filthy spaces. The creatures use the rag piles as beds. At the present time, **6 dark creepers** occupy these quarters. The dark creepers have no concept of privacy and personal property. They simply crawl into an unoccupied mushroom and fall asleep whenever they are tired. Without their dark stalker masters, these lesser humanoids are inherently chaotic and disorganized. Each individual occupies his own mushroom, so there is a 67% chance of encountering one of the dark creepers within their abode. There is also a 50% chance that the dark creeper is asleep. If the characters attack one of the dark creepers, or the creatures otherwise become aware of the characters' presence, they shout to get the others' attention. The dark creepers never surrender, and they have no useful information.

Dark Creepers (6): HD 1+1; **HP** 9, 8x3, 6x2; **AC** 7[12] or 0[19] in darkness; **Atk** dagger (1d4 plus poison); **Move** 9; **Save** 17; **AL** C; **CL/XP** 3/60; **Special:** create special darkness (50ft radius, 1/day, extinguish normal light sources, magical light sources save or extinguished, darkvision fails), death-flash (10ft radius, save or blinded for 1d6 rounds), level 4 thief. (***Monstrosities*** 83)
> **Thieving Skills:** Climb 88%, Tasks/Traps 30%, Hear 4 in 6, Hide 25%, Silent 35%, Locks 25%.
> **Equipment:** dagger, 3 doses of black smear poison (save or lose 1d2 strength for 2d6–1 rounds, death at 0 strength).

Treasure: As previously mentioned, the dark creepers do not collect items for themselves. Still, characters can locate 3d6 x 10gp scattered within one of the mushrooms among the piles of rags and other filth inside of the crude homes. However, the horrid stench is so strong within these confined areas that a character searching through one of the mushrooms must make a successful saving throw to avoid becoming nauseated for 1d4 minutes afterward.

D8. Food Production

A roughly 2-foot-high stone wall spans the chamber's narrowest section. Large mushrooms and clustered bunches of tendril-shaped fungi grow from the walls, floor and ceiling. Various sized worms ranging from tiny earthworms to 1-foot-long night crawlers burrow through the loose soil and refuse littering the floor.

The dark folk subsist predominately on a diet of fungi and worms. The primitive plants are mostly edible with the exception of three striped toadstools. The worms are edible and harmless. They pose no danger to the characters.

D9. Rag Production

Fungi attached to the walls radiate an eerie phosphorescent glow that bathes the damp natural cavern in a violet haze. Tall, unusual flowering plants grow in black, potted soil contained within a walled enclosure along the chamber's edges. Two long poles attached to spinning wheels and a stone vat of brackish water take up the balance of the cramped room's space.

The dark folk grow and harvest a subterranean species of the flax plant in this illuminated, underground greenhouse. The poles and spinning wheel are part of a distaff, a tool used to dry and separate flax fibers. In addition, the stone vat is used to soak the plant stalks after they have already been dried.

D10. Metalworking Chamber

Large chunks of metallic ore and limestone are piled upon the floor near a partially covered stone pit filled with charcoal. An anvil rests near the apparent heat source, and several metalworking tools such as small hammers and tongs are strewn about the floor. A weapons rack against the near wall contains an assortment of daggers and a handful of short swords.

The dark folk's rudimentary metalworking skills pale in comparison to the dwarves' mastery of the craft. The sly humanoids only use the chunks of iron ore adjacent to the primitive blast furnace to create their daggers, short swords, tools, nails, and other mundane items. Pieces of limestone mixed among the iron ore are necessary to separate the slag from the iron. An examination of the charcoal pit determines that the dark folk used the apparatus within the last several weeks apparently to forge the daggers on the adjacent rack.

The dark folk's resident metalworker is the dark stalker **Ruvgarn**. He toils in this hot chamber along with **2 dark creepers**. The apprentice magic-user seems an odd choice to forge mundane metal items and weapons. Unfortunately, he is more skilled than anyone else in the complex. The dark stalker has an array of spells and spell-like abilities at his disposal. Unlike most dark folk, Ruvgarn does not plunge the crowded area into darkness. Instead, he relies upon his *wand of magic missiles* and his spells to damage the characters. Ruvgarn refuses to surrender or retreat. If forcibly compelled to provide information, he reveals the same details as his dark stalker counterpart in **Area D6**. Otherwise, he and the dark creepers fight to the death.

Ruvgarn, Dark Stalker: HD 7; **HP** 49; **AC** 8[11] or 2[17] (missile) and 4[15] (melee) from *shield* spell or 0[19] in darkness; **Atk** +1 dagger (1d4+1 plus poison), sling (1d4); **Move** 12; **Save** 8 (+1, ring); **AL** C; **CL/XP** 9/1100; **Special:** +2 save vs. spells, wands or staffs, create special darkness (50ft radius, 3/day, extinguish normal light sources, magical light sources save or extinguished, darkvision fails), death-flash (40ft radius, save or 3d6 damage), spells (4/2/2). (***Monstrosities*** 84)
> **Spells:** 1st—*charm person, protection from evil, shield, sleep*; 2nd—*invisibility, phantasmal force*; 3rd—*dispel magic, lightning bolt.*
> **Equipment:** +1 dagger, sling, 20 sling stones, *wand of magic missile* (18 charges), *ring of protection +1*, scroll (*monster summoning I*), 2 doses of black smear poison, blacksmithing tools.

Dark Creepers (2): HD 1+1; **HP** 8, 7; **AC** 7[12] or 0[19] in darkness; **Atk** dagger (1d4 plus poison); **Move** 9; **Save** 17; **AL** C; **CL/XP** 3/60; **Special:** create special darkness (50ft radius, 1/day, extinguish normal light sources, magical light sources save or extinguished, darkvision fails), death-flash (10ft radius, save or blinded for 1d6 rounds), level 4 thief. (*Monstrosities* 83)

> **Thieving Skills:** Climb 88%, Tasks/Traps 30%, Hear 4 in 6, Hide 25%, Silent 35%, Locks 25%.
> **Equipment:** dagger, 3 doses of black smear poison (save or lose 1d2 strength for 2d6–1 rounds, death at 0 strength).

Treasure: There are sixteen daggers and eight short swords on the weapons rack, though none of them is magical.

D11. Iron Mine

Large gouges mar the floor of a rough-hewn corridor that sharply descends into the earth.

Also not renowned as miners, the dark folk simply kept burrowing into the ground until they struck iron ore deposits. The tunnel descends at a 30-degree angle, but it is still easy to negotiate. As their needs for the metal are not particularly great, the tunnel abruptly ends at a rich vein of the versatile metal.

D12. Guard Chamber

Mounds of filthy rags and tattered linens lie scattered upon the floor. The stench of sweat and rancid food fills the air.

Though confident in his divine mistress's master scheme, Rogvörn must take at least some precautions against an assault on the dark folk's vulnerable underbelly. With that in mind, he stationed **1 dark stalker** and **6 dark creepers** to protect against this contingency. The dark stalker keeps his subservient kin on their proverbial toes. At the first sign of trouble, the group's leader uses his *darkness* ability to shroud the chamber in blackness. The dark folk continue attacking until slain. They do not speak to the characters until compelled to do otherwise. The dark creepers are blissfully in the dark about Rogvörn's machinations. On the other hand, the dark stalker is intimately familiar with Mirkeer's grand plan. He has the same information as his counterpart in **Area D6**.

Dark Creepers (6): HD 1+1; HP 8x2, 7x3, 5; AC 7[12] or 0[19] in darkness; Atk dagger (1d4 plus poison); Move 9; Save 17; AL C; CL/XP 3/60; Special: backstab (x2), create special darkness (50ft radius, 1/day, extinguish normal light sources, magical light sources save or extinguished, darkvision fails), death-flash (10ft radius, save or blinded for 1d6 rounds), level 4 thief. (*Monstrosities* 83)

> **Thieving Skills:** Climb 88%, Tasks/Traps 30%, Hear 4 in 6, Hide 25%, Silent 35%, Locks 25%.
> **Equipment:** dagger, 3 doses of black smear poison (save or lose 1d2 strength for 2d6–1 rounds, death at 0 strength).

Dark Stalker: HD 6+2; HP 40; AC 7[12] or 0[19] in darkness; Atk short sword (1d6 plus poison); Move 12; Save 11; AL C; CL/XP 8/800; Special: backstab (x2), create special darkness (50ft radius, 3/day, extinguish normal light sources, magical light sources save or extinguished, darkvision fails), death-flash (40ft radius, save or 3d6 damage), level 4 thief. (*Monstrosities* 84)

> **Thieving Skills:** Climb 88%, Tasks/Traps 30%, Hear 4 in 6, Hide 25%, Silent 35%, Locks 25%.
> **Equipment:** leather armor, 2 short swords, 6 doses of black smear poison (save or lose 1d2 strength for 2d6–1 rounds, death at 0 strength), *potion of extra healing*, pouch with 4 rubies (250gp each).

Treasure: The dark creepers have a total of 16 moonstones worth 50gp each.

D13. Antechamber

The corridor opens into an antechamber that ends in three identical doors crafted from hardened fungus.

The antechamber represents the dark folk's last line of defense against intruders. One of the three doors leads to the heart of the complex, whereas the other two doors unleash nasty surprises designed to slay intruders. The doors are exactly the same size, shape and appearance. There is relatively little traffic passing in and out of the complex's heart, so there are no telltale signs that one door or section of the floor appears to get more use than the others. In fact, the dark folk deliberately walk up to all three doors to give the impression that they are used in an equal fashion. However, the doors leading into **Area D13A** and **Area D13B** are less worn than the remaining door. Likewise, there is more foot traffic in front of the door leading into the heart of the dark folk's complex. They also imbedded a thin sheet of lead in each portal and the surrounding thresholds to thwart spells such as *ESP*, *clairvoyance* or *clairaudience*. The metal does nothing to alter the doors' structural integrity. They still yield to physical force in the same manner as the other doors on this level.

D13A: What Lurks Above

A wide, rough-hewn stone corridor turns west and then bends sharply to the north.

The ordinary looking chamber and passageway are intended to appear normal to hide the **ceiling lurker** concealed upon the ceiling. The nearly mindless predator camouflages itself into the surrounding environment, making it appear to be just part of the cavern. The lurker above encompasses the entire ceiling from the door to the point where the corridor turns north. The creature drops down from its hiding place as soon as a character passes through the door and sets foot in the chamber.

Ceiling Lurker: HD 10; HP 67; AC 6[13]; Atk crush (1d6); Move 1 (fly 7); Save 5; AL N; CL/XP 12/2,000; Special: smother (1d6 damage per round, death in 1d4+1 rounds). (*Monstrosities* 304)

D13B. Twilight of the Mushrooms

Ten six-inch high, purplish-black mushrooms are spread across the floor, walls and ceiling of a small alcove.

The resident fungi are **twilight mushrooms**, a deadly hazard that plagues underground explorers.

Twilight Mushrooms

The Tome of Horrors Complete 579

Twilight mushrooms are purplish-black mushrooms about 4in to 6in in height. They grow in patches of 5–10 mushrooms and are found only in damp, dark underground areas. Twilight mushrooms sense vibrations and burst forth a cloud of noxious and choking dust when a living creature comes within 10ft of a patch. Creatures within the area must succeed on a saving throw or take 2d6 points of damage. One minute later another saving throw must be made — even by those who succeeded on the first one — to avoid another 1d6 points of damage. Whether or not the saves are successful, a creature is disabled for 2d4 rounds from fits of choking and coughing. Such a creature can take no action other than to defend itself. Sunlight renders twilight mushrooms dormant, and cold instantly destroys them.

D13C. Corridor

The rough-hewn stone corridor splits in two. One passageway leads south and ends in a fungal door. The other continues to the west and also ends in a fungal door.

This corridor leads into the heart of the dark folk's complex. The southern corridor opens into **Area D14** and the western passage takes the characters to **Area D15**.

D14. Charnel Dump

Pieces of bone, rotting flesh, and even a mummified eye are visible among the soiled fabrics that create an uneven surface on the floor of this chamber.

The dark folk toss the corpses of dead foes onto the floor of this chamber to keep them out from underfoot. Over the decades, there has been a considerable accumulation here. The floor is stacked so heavily rotting bodies that the entire chamber is considered to be difficult terrain.

D15. Meeting Area

Eight grotesque statues apparently carved from fungi, molds and mushrooms form a perimeter around a stone table surrounded by eight toadstool chairs. The sculptures depict a winged humanoid with clawed hands and feet as well as a toothy maw. A highly detailed map covers much of the vaguely oval table. Phosphorescent mold clinging to the walls bathes the entire chamber in dim, green light.

Rogvörn conveyed his grand strategy to his counterparts in this meeting room. The map covering the table details much of the Stoneheart Mountains, though it is centered on Tyr Whin. Several lines drawn onto the map indicate a large force moving from the hobgoblin citadel of Exor toward Clan Craenog's remote outpost. In addition, a note scrawled onto the margins states, "*B to move half of force to Erod Flan.*" This message refers to Blassian's plan to transfer half of Tyr Whin's defenders to Erod Flan after the royal family's demise. The incriminating statement confirms the traitorous dwarf's involvement in the dark folk's plans.

The statues surrounding the table represent the extent of the dark folk's artistic abilities. Five of the gruesome statues are inanimate objects carved from an amalgamation of mold, fungi and mushrooms. Interspersed among these statues are **3 fungus gargoyles** that remain completely motionless until the characters attack one of them or the characters come within 10ft. The dim, phosphorescent glow emanating from the moldy walls allows them to see in this area. They attack all living creatures other than dark folk and their bloody bones ally. When they spring to life, each releases its frightening breath weapon. After expending their breath weapons, the creatures attack the intruders with their claws. With nowhere left to retreat, the monstrous plants fight to the bitter end.

Fungus Gargoyles (3): HD 5; **HP** 37, 34, 31; **AC** 4[15]; **Atk** 2 claws (1d6); **Move** 14 (fly 18); **Save** 12; **AL** N; **CL/XP** 5/240; **Special:** fungus breath (every 1d4 rounds, 30ft cone, 1d6 damage, save avoids), stench (10ft radius, save or retch violently for 1 round). (**The Tome of Horrors Complete** 263)

D16. Living Quarters

Four upright stone beds with footrests and sinewy straps are positioned against the walls of a spotless chamber. A finely crafted shield rests upon a stone pedestal.

The 4 fastidious dark stalkers sleep in an upright position, affixing themselves to these uncomfortable beds with straps fashioned from plant matter. The room is currently unoccupied. In contrast to the dark creepers' abodes, there is not even a speck of dust or dirt on the floor.

Treasure: The quartet saved the *+2 shield* as a trophy from their first encounter with the dwarves.

D17. Rogvörn's Laboratory

The stench of burning sulfur and the malodorous wisps of smoke overwhelm the senses. Beakers and jars cover a fungal table abutting the near wall where a lithe, milky-white 6-foot-tall humanoid clad in black robes feverishly concocts a volatile creation. Two small humanoids cloaked in filthy, disgusting rags futilely attempt to assist him in this endeavor. A bizarre creature that resembles a skeletal human torso cloaked in roiling shadows that obscures its innards, but not its shape, oversees the frenetic operation. A stone statue of a beautiful and mysterious woman stands just inside of the fungal door. Obsidian chips inlaid into the floor create a crude mosaic that looks like a black glove. A bookcase containing several dozen dog-eared tomes abuts the south wall.

The statue depicts Mirkeer. As with most dark folk artwork, the technique is rather poor. The obsidian mosaic on the floor represents the goddess' symbol.

Shortly after the detonation, **Rogvörn** cast a *commune* spell to determine whether the plan succeeded. Based upon the answer he received from his divine mistress, he is fairly certain that the methane explosion did not fulfill its intended purpose. In light of that dire information, he frantically tries to create another bomb. The novice alchemist also constructs a crude device that serves as a triggering mechanism. The detonator is nothing more than a merchant's scale, a funnel, and a bucket of dirt. The bomb flask is placed precariously on the edge of a tall stone column. The merchant's scale is placed on an adjacent column. The dirt slowly passes through the narrow funnel's neck and onto one end of merchant's scale much like sand passes through an hourglass. When the added weight is enough to move the opposite arm, it knocks the bomb flask off the adjacent pedestal causing it to fall to the ground and burst into flames, thus igniting the methane gas.

The dark caller's laboratory is very basic and in poor condition. There are eleven jars and beakers on the table along with several other alchemical substances. The **2 dark creepers** assisting him rush from one end of the table to the other in a feeble attempt to please their overlord. The books on the shelf opposite the laboratory table predominantly discuss alchemy and other pseudo sciences.

Rogvörn, Dark Stalker: HD 9; **HP** 68; **AC** 3[16] or 0[19] in darkness; **Atk** +2 *freezing dagger* (1d4+2 plus 1d6 cold); **Move** 12; **Save** 5 (+1, ring); **AL** C; **CL/XP** 11/1700; **Special:** +2 save vs. spells, wands or staffs, create special darkness (50ft radius, 3/day, extinguish normal light sources, magical light sources save or extinguished, darkvision fails), death-flash (40ft radius, save or 3d6 damage), spells (4/3/3/2/1). (**Monstrosities** 84)

Spells: 1st—*cause light wounds, charm person, detect magic, magic missile;* 2nd—*hold person, strength, web;* 3rd—*dispel magic, lightning bolt, speak with dead;* 4th—*cause serious wounds, confusion;* 5th—*commune.*

Equipment: *bracers of defense AC 4[15], +2 freezing dagger, ring of protection +1, scroll (monster summoning II),* 2 doses of black smear poison.

Bloody Bones, Emissary of Mirkeer: HD 5; **HP** 34; **AC** 3[16]; **Atk** 4 tendrils (1d4 plus poison), 2 claws (1d6); **Move** 12; **Save** 12; **AL** C; **CL/XP** 7/600; **Special:** resist fire (50%), slippery (escape confinement), tendrils (after hit, save or be held and pulled toward creature; each tendril has 10hp, AC 3[16]). (*The Tome of Horrors Complete* 63)

Dark Creepers (2): HD 1+1; **HP** 9, 7; **AC** 7[12] or 0[19] in darkness; **Atk** dagger (1d4 plus poison); **Move** 9; **Save** 17; **AL** C; **CL/XP** 3/60; **Special:** create special darkness (50ft radius, 1/day, extinguish normal light sources, magical light sources save or extinguished, darkvision fails), death-flash (10ft radius, save or blinded for 1d6 rounds), level 4 thief. (*Monstrosities* 83)

> **Thieving Skills:** Climb 88%, Tasks/Traps 30%, Hear 4 in 6, Hide 25%, Silent 35%, Locks 25%.
> **Equipment:** dagger, 3 doses of black smear poison (save or lose 1d2 strength for 2d6–1 rounds, death at 0 strength).

Tactics: Rogvörn is so immersed in his work that he barely notices the characters' intrusion unless otherwise alerted by their failed efforts to open the fungal door or their actions. Mirkeer's **bloody bones** emissary is much more attentive. It almost certainly reacts to the unwelcome interruption. Rogvörn does not plunge the area into darkness, as the dark folk do elsewhere. Even when faced with imminent defeat, Rogvörn refuses to surrender. He repeatedly boasts that the dwarves' time is at hand, and that Tyr Whin's imminent defeat is the first of many for Clan Craenog. He divulges nothing else of significance during his tirade. If the characters compel him to speak against his will, he reveals Mirkeer's involvement, Blassian's treachery, and Grugdour's role in the grand scheme.

The bloody bones never communicates with the characters during the melee. It strikes with its tendrils to pull characters toward its claws. The dark creepers act as fodder, always sacrificing themselves. The humanoids happily die in the service of their dark stalker master.

Treasure: Rogvörn's collection of alchemy equipment, raw ingredients and books are worth a meager 50gp. Otherwise, nothing of value is here.

D18. Detonation Site

> Warm, foul-smelling air fills the featureless cavern.

Piles of loose stones and debris block the corridor leading from **Area D12** to the detonation site proper. Likewise, massive quantities of rubble fill the entire cavern. The passageway connecting the dark folk's complex with the thane's banquet hall is 80ft below that room's floor. In order to focus the explosion's force upward, the dark folk assembled a conical tower of coal in the center of the empty chamber. Their design strategy explains why the crater continued to smolder after the explosion and the immense quantity of debris present within the hole in spite of the limited damage dealt to the dwarves' expertly crafted structure. After the blast, the inverted funnel collapsed, and the resulting debris filled the recesses to create a relatively uniform surface 20ft below the banquet hall floor.

If the characters somehow remove the rubble, they can locate components from the ignition device. The characters inexplicably find pieces of a merchant's scale and shards from a ceramic vessel. If the characters already explored **Area D16**, the items appear identical to those that Rogvörn is using to build another detonation trigger.

D19. Secondary Detonation Site

> A thick, uneven layer of guano covers the floor and every other surface within an expansive cavern with an 80-foot-high ceiling. The stench fills the air and spills down the adjoining corridor. A poorly designed mine cart with a lopsided axle and vaguely round wheels sits near the entrance. The piercing shriek of metal striking stone reverberates throughout the expansive chamber. A massive 60-foot-high mound of rock rich with coal deposits and coated with layers of disgusting excrement occupies the cavern's center.

A small colony of bats clings to the ceiling and the surrounding walls. The animals are harmless and pose no threat to the adventurers. The bats feed on the crickets and other small insects that crawl along the guano-covered floor. The dark folk collected the mammals from other parts of their complex and the quartz mine and concentrated them in this chamber to rapidly increase the production of methane gas within the confined space. Therefore, the chances of encountering a pocket of methane gas or bad air increase fourfold in this room. Still, the quantities are not sufficient yet to create an explosion capable of destroying the dwarves' aboveground structures.

Though he agreed not to attack the dwarves again once Blassian assumes control over Clan Craenog, the treacherous Rogvörn still longs to destroy his hated enemies once and for all. The failed attempt to eradicate the high thane's family merely accelerated his plans. To that end, **6 dark creepers** toil in the spacious cavern, using their metal picks to remove stone from the coal deposits. The laborers then dump the excess stones and rocks onto the mine cart and roll them over to **Area D20**. When they notice the intrusion, the weary dark creepers drop their picks and immediately attack the characters. Like the rest of their kin, these devoutly loyal dark folk fight to the bitter end. They have no knowledge of their master's plans.

Dark Creepers (6): HD 1+1; **HP** 9, 8x3, 7x2; **AC** 7[12] or 0[19] in darkness; **Atk** dagger (1d4 plus poison); **Move** 9; **Save** 17; **AL** C; **CL/XP** 3/60; **Special:** create special darkness (50ft radius, 1/day, extinguish normal light sources, magical light sources save or extinguished, darkvision fails), death-flash (10ft radius, save or blinded for 1d6 rounds), level 4 thief. (*Monstrosities* 83)

> **Thieving Skills:** Climb 88%, Tasks/Traps 30%, Hear 4 in 6, Hide 25%, Silent 35%, Locks 25%.
> **Equipment:** dagger, 3 doses of black smear poison (save or lose 1d2 strength for 2d6–1 rounds, death at 0 strength).

D20. Acid Bath

> Five metal barrels filled with clear, viscous liquid are scattered throughout the cramped room.

The dark creepers dump the rocks and stone cleared from **Area D19** and prior to that **Area D18** into the metal barrels filled with specialized acid. The corrosive substance is better attuned to dissolving rock and stone than it is to destroying organic material. It deals 1-1/2 times its normal damage to rock and stone (including creatures with the earth descriptor), and only half damage to organic matter, including undead creatures.

D21. Watery Cavern

A damp chill fills the stagnant air. Water slowly drips from the 40-foot-high ceiling and collects in four large pools scattered throughout the cavern. The glint of golden nuggets is visible beneath the water's surface. Numerous stalactites resembling stony tendrils cling to the ceiling, though no stalagmites cover the floor. Instead, a colorful assortment of wild fungi grow along the gravely edges surrounding the underground pools.

The dark folk originally intended to use this chamber to burrow into Erod Flan and attack their foes from below, but they abandoned that notion once they struck water. Instead, they lured **2 tendriculos** that they found in another part of their complex into this natural cavern where they could feast on the mineral-rich water without harassing the dark folk. As an aside, they also believed that the golden nuggets in the water might entice adventurers to explore the chamber. The tendriculos remain close to the edge of the pools and blend in well with the other strange indigenous plants and fungi.

Tendriculos (2): HD 8; **HP** 57, 53; **AC** 4[15]; Atk 2 tendrils (1d6), bite (2d6); **Move** 9; **Save** 8; **AL** N; **CL/XP** 9/1100; **Special:** swallow whole (2 tendrils strike, save or swallowed, 1d6 damage per round). (**Monstrosities** 468)

Tactics: The tendriculos rush characters if they come within 15ft. If the characters attack the tendriculos from a distance of greater than 20ft, the plants close the gap separating them from their attackers. The monsters fight until destroyed.

Treasure: The tendriculos do not accumulate any riches. However, the golden nuggets in the pools are real. Each of the pools contains 2d4 small nuggets worth 10gp each and 1d4 larger chunks of the precious metal worth 50gp each.

Concluding the Adventure

The high thane and his surviving family members are eternally grateful to the characters for eradicating the dark folk and thwarting their plans to destroy Erod Flan. Fearful of another incursion from their hated foes, the dwarves permanently station a small military force in the tunnels beneath their capital. In the meantime, the dwarves' master stonemasons and artisans start to rebuild what the malevolent humanoids destroyed.

While there is no love lost for the slain dark folk, the traitorous Blassian poses a different dilemma. The popular dwarf's treason comes as a shock to all those that knew him, especially Kaelan. If he survived his encounter with the characters, the victims' families demand justice. Surprisingly, the plot's intended target acts as the voice of reason. The high thane is willing to spare Blassian's wretched life and sentence him to 100 years of hard labor, if his distant cousin reveals the intricate details of his dark patron's plans. In spite of his devotion to Mirkeer, the egotistical Blassian would prefer meeting his proverbial maker sometime in the distant future. In exchange for his life, the dwarf conspirator willingly reveals that the hobgoblin overlord Grugdour plans an imminent assault against Tyr Whin. In addition, he was supposed to transfer roughly half of Tyr Whin's garrison to Erod Flan in order to bolster the capital's defenses in the wake of the dark folk's explosion. If he is compelled to speak against his will, Blassian also discloses that the hobgoblins infected the outpost with a debilitating strain of a disease they crafted to specifically affect dwarves.

Blassian's information and other clues gathered during the characters' exploration of the dark folk's lair all point to the inevitable conclusion that the hobgoblins of Exor are marching toward the distant citadel of Tyr Whin. The high thane's attention now shifts from saving his capital to defending his clan peaks against the hobgoblin threat. The tactically astute ruler realizes that a large force marching through the low-ways of his clan peaks will take time and could be entering an ambush prepared by his enemies. He needs a small, fast advance force to clear the way and begin preparing the defenses of Tyr Whin while the larger force gathers and begins its slower march. For this he turns to the characters again and beseeches them to lend whatever aid they can to Tyr Whin.

Erod Flan

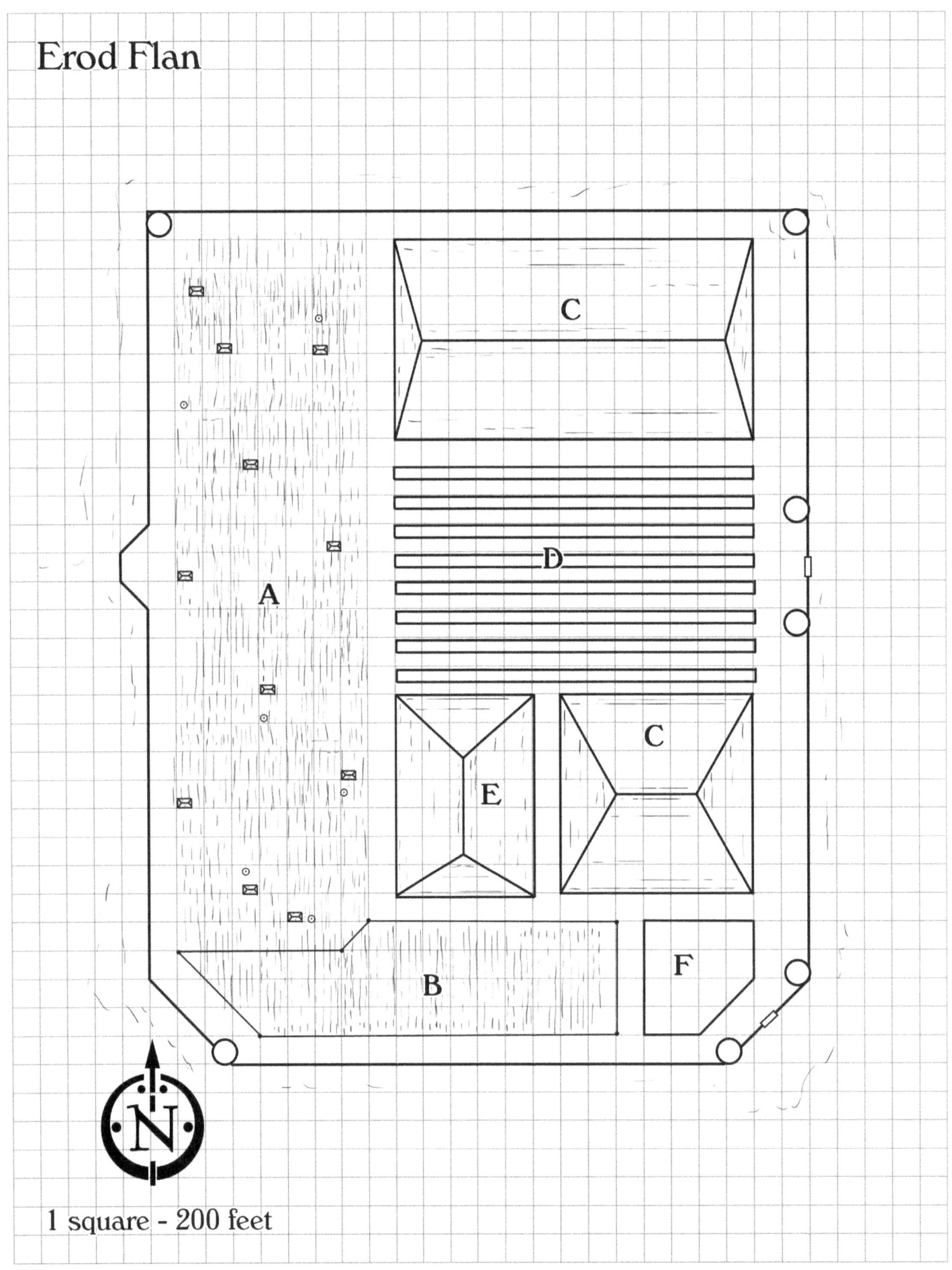

1 square - 200 feet

Quartz Mine   1 square - 10 feet

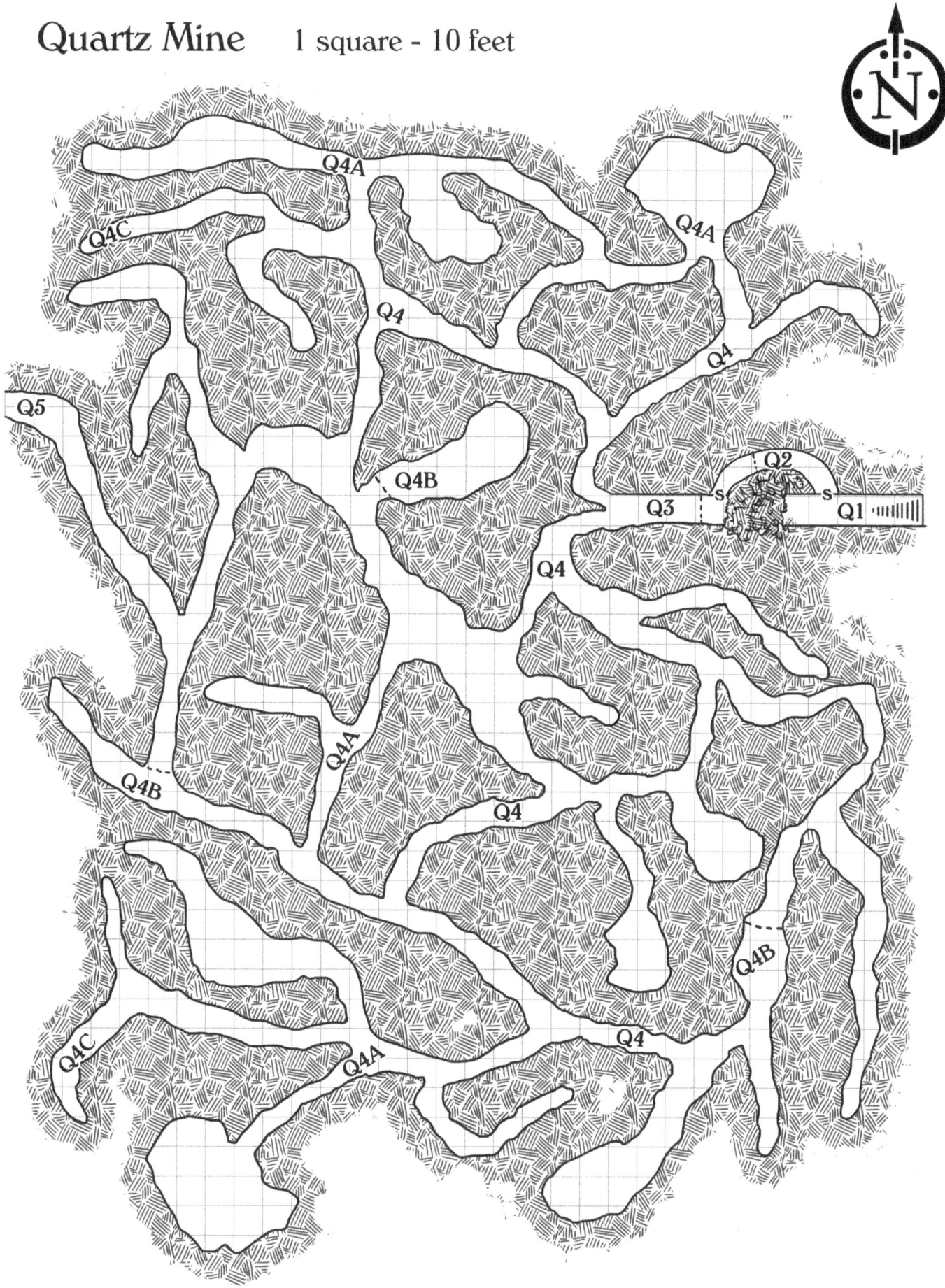

1 square - 20 feet

Dark Folk Complex
1 square - 5 feet

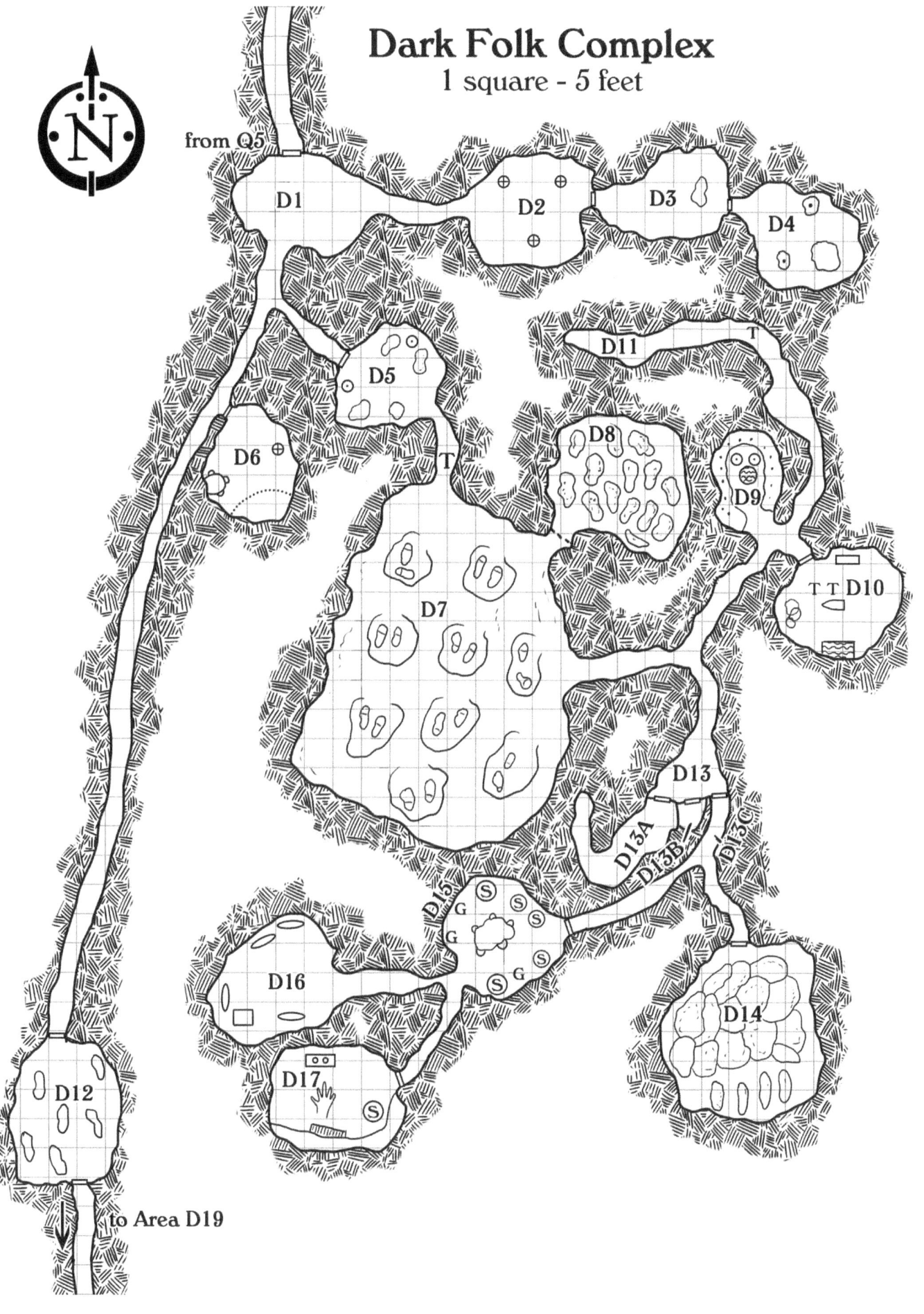

Explosion Site
1 square - 10 feet

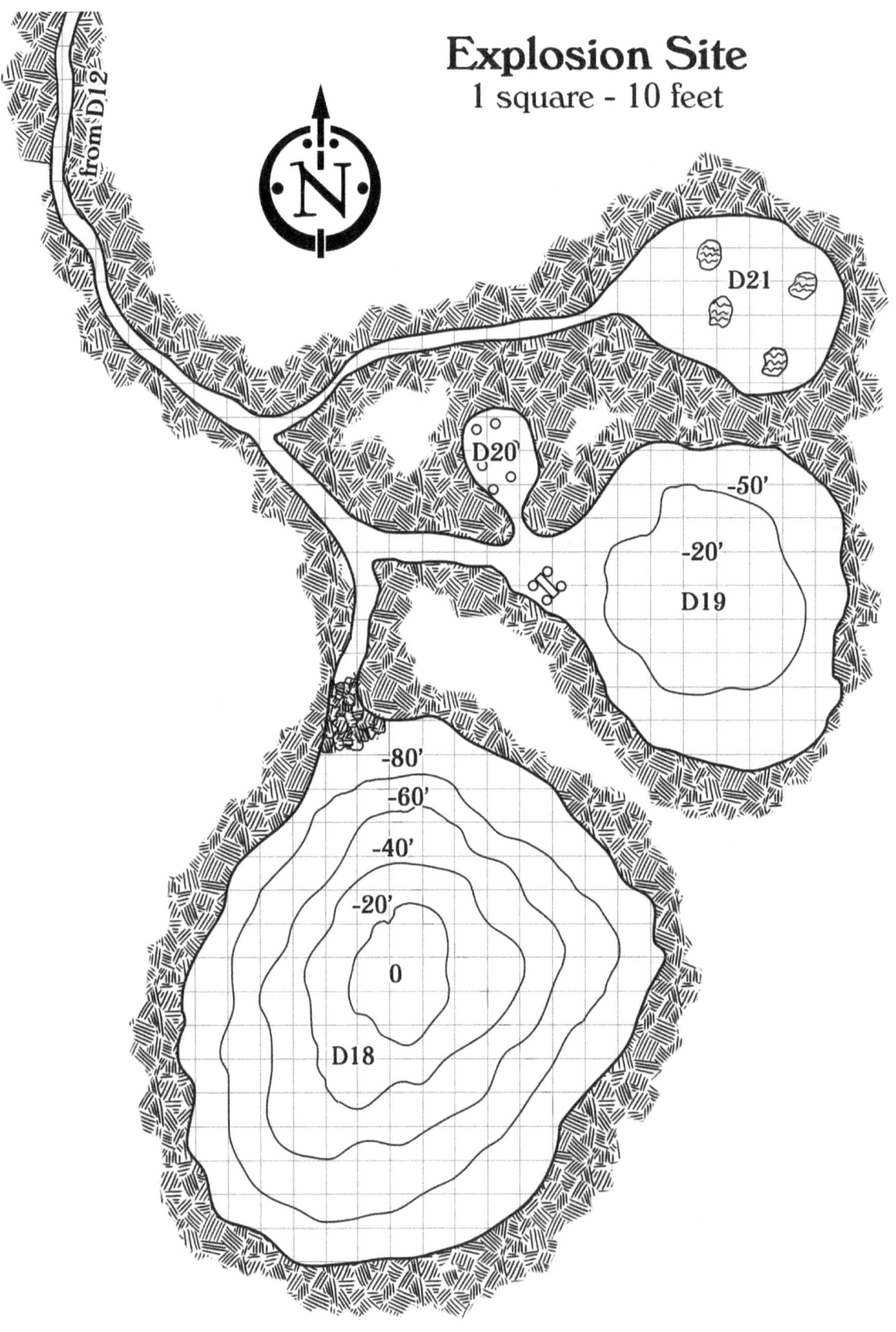